ONE NIGHT WITH A DUKE

ERICA RIDLEY

Wish Upon a Duke

Never Say Duke

Dukes, Actually

The Duke's Bride

The Duke's Embrace

The Duke's Desire

Dawn With a Duke

One Night With a Duke

Ten Days With a Duke

Forever Your Duke

Gothic Love Stories:

Too Wicked to Kiss

Too Sinful to Deny

Too Tempting to Resist

Too Wanton to Wed

Too Brazen to Bite

Magic & Mayhem:

Kissed by Magic

Must Love Magic

Smitten by Magic

Welcome to Christmas!

Our picturesque village is nestled around Marlowe Castle, high atop the gorgeous mountain we call home. Cressmouth is best known for our year-round Yuletide cheer. Here, we're family.

The legend of our twelve dukes? Absolutely true! But they may not always be who—or what—one might expect…

~

CHAPTER 1

December 1814

 r. Jonathan MacLean *could* have spent the two-hour journey from Eyemouth, Scotland to Cressmouth, England tucked safely into the relative warmth of the hackney coach he'd hired, but where was the pleasure in that?

Perched out here with his driver, Mr. Beattie, no foggy window pane stood between Jonathan and the rolling vista. All around them, snow-covered hills topped a sea of frost-speckled evergreens. He was en route to adventure—once again!—and he didn't want to miss a single moment of it.

After two hours together, the hackney driver had warmed to his unconventional client.

"Well..." Beattie squinted into the wind. "I wouldn't gad about crying, 'A pox on raisins!' but there's a limit to how many a man ought to find in his biscuit, isn't there?"

"Pah!" Jonathan said. "I like biscuits with raisins, biscuits without raisins, bread with raisins, bread without raisins, cakes with raisins, cakes without raisins, a bowl full of nothing *but* raisins..."

The list of things Jonathan liked was infinite. The right attitude limited opportunities for disappointment. It was difficult for things not to go one's way, when one was determined to like *all* the ways.

Beattie was the best driver a traveler could hope to be paired with. He hadn't objected in the least when Jonathan promised to triple his earnings if he shared his rickety, wind-whipped perch with a stranger.

To fill the dead air, they'd shared their life stories—Jonathan's began when he was sixteen, no sense dredging up memories from his childhood —and were now on to arbitrary preferences, which was exactly the sort of easy, superficial, boundless topic he liked best.

"Towns," said Beattie with a sly look in his eye. "As a traveling peddler who's been to every corner of Britain, there *must* be some place you refuse to return to."

Jonathan wasn't precisely a peddler, but he was unquestionably a traveler, and it was this topic he'd expected to be peppered with questions about upon declaring himself an open book and taking the controversial stance of not disliking anything. That they'd covered raisins and ragwort and kite-flying on windy days spoke highly of Beattie's creativity. Too many people only concentrated on the obvious.

"I refuse to return to *all* places," Jonathan replied cheerfully. "Not because I've disliked them, but because there are so many more I haven't seen. One week, that's my rule. Less, if I can help it. Then it's on to the next town, and the next adventure. I'm the luckiest man alive!"

Beattie stared at him, aghast. "You haven't a *home?*"

Jonathan ignored the familiar ache he kept buried deep inside. He'd had a home once. A mother who rarely spoke to him. A father who never came round. Four walls that provided no comfort at all. Yuletides spent staring out of the window, dreaming of a place where he would be wanted.

But dreams were for children.

Life had taught Jonathan it was safer never to get attached in the first place.

"How can I pick a place to stay still," he pointed out reasonably, "until I've experienced everything, to know for certain which I'll like best?"

Beattie's wind-chapped lips gaped.

"You should try it," Jonathan suggested. "You said you'd never been out of Scotland, and now here you are, on holiday in England!"

Beattie gazed doubtfully at the endless drifts of snow encroaching on the winding road.

"I'm not on holiday," he reminded Jonathan. "You paid me handsomely to make this journey."

"Was it not enough?" Jonathan pulled several more freezing guineas from his coin purse and dropped them into Beattie's gaping pocket, heavy from all the other coins Jonathan had foisted upon him. "There, now you can be on holiday, as well. Although I should confess that I am always on holiday and not on holiday at the same time."

Beattie's frost-tipped lashes blinked. "Your confessions always leave me more confused than when I started."

Jonathan beamed at him. "Part of the fun, isn't it? A body might think—"

But the words froze in his throat like so many icicles. A festive crimson sign rose like a beacon just ahead:

Welcome to Christmas!

"Cressmouth," Jonathan muttered. "The village is called *Cressmouth*."

"Aye, well," said Beattie. "It might be *named* Cressmouth, but even I know it's *called* 'Christmas' by everyone between Shetland and Cornwall. Isn't that why you're here? Everyone adores Christmas!"

Jonathan would rather there be no Christmas at all.

"What's that?" he said, pointing a leather-clad finger at a telltale waft of smoke rising from a gray blur of a brick house in the middle of a large field.

Between the falling snow and the corkscrew path up the evergreen-furred mountain, the village had been completely hidden from view until, suddenly, it wasn't.

This was interesting, indeed! H-A-R-P was just visible on a thick wooden sign blanketed in snow. A stud farm, by the looks of it. One of the most famous in England, to be specific. Everyone had heard of the Harpers.

One of their horses was of royal caliber, according to the broadsheets, and was the most in-demand of all the fine blood horses in Britain. No lesser personage than the Prince Regent had attempted to purchase it, but he *hadn't* been able to, which only made the horse quintuple in value and the Harpers all the more infamous.

"Look!" A horse and rider cut across the Harpers' snow-covered fields.

"I can't look," Beattie grumbled. "I can't even see the road with you leaning past me like an overeager puppy. If you were *inside* the carriage, you could look out of the window and—"

"Nothing interesting happens whilst cloistered somewhere," Jonathan scolded him.

He twisted backward onto the perch, his frozen knees balancing on the tattered squab, just in time for the rider to come within shouting distance.

"Ho, there!" he called out. "Lovely horse you've got! I'll buy it from you!"

"What would you do with a horse," Beattie asked, "when you haven't even got a house?"

"Give it to you," Jonathan replied sensibly. "What a wonderful story it will make! 'How did you enjoy your time in Cressmouth?' they'll ask—"

"*Christmas*," Beattie corrected. "It's called *Christmas*."

Jonathan *wanted* to like everything. He *tried* to like everything. But some things...

He continued on, ignoring Beattie's interruption. "'Och, you know, boring old seasonal nonsense,' most people would reply. 'Bought a watercolor of a pine tree, in case I forget what one looks like when I've gone back home.' But not me, Beattie, and not you! 'Bought a horse,' I'll say, 'from the famous Harper stud farm. Gave it to my hack driver. Hope he likes it better than raisins.' And you'll say—"

"I won't say a blessed thing," Beattie said, "because that gentleman didn't even look up when you called, so I daresay you won't be buying any horses."

"Perhaps not *today*," Jonathan allowed, "but anything could happen tomorrow. The best adventures are unpredictable."

"I predict I won't be here to find out," Beattie said. "Once you alight at your cottage, I shall turn around and go home. You might not believe in permanence, but I've got a wife who'll be keeping supper warm for me. Something to consider."

"Pah," said Jonathan. "If I can't decide on a home until I've seen them all, how am I supposed to take a wife? Do you know how many more women there are than cities and hamlets? Even if I limited myself to conversing five minutes with each one, I'd never meet them all in a hundred years."

"You don't have to meet them all," Beattie said in exasperation. "Find a good one and keep her."

"I don't want a good lass," Jonathan explained. "I want a splendid lass. I want the *best* lass. Nothing else will do."

"And 'nothing' is what you'll end up with," Beattie predicted. "I hope you like suppers alone."

"Be *alone?*" Jonathan clutched his chest. "I've taken every meal with a different person for as long as I can remember."

Well, for as long as he'd been on the road—which was the only bit he chose to remember.

Not that Beattie was listening. He stared openmouthed at the majestic castle soaring up into the sky at the top of the mountain. It looked like something out of a fairy book. Or it would, if it weren't surrounded by a living black moat of holiday-makers in smart carriages, and swarming pedestrians in bright-colored woolen caps.

"Turn here," Jonathan commanded, shaking out the small hand-drawn map that had come with his invitation. "To the right, past the pond, curve about until... here!"

One might not think a village of a thousand souls would require much in the way of maps, but the Duke of Nottingvale was nothing if not thorough. It was a quality Jonathan very much admired, and it boded splendidly for their upcoming business partnership—*if* the presentation went as planned.

He leapt to the ground the moment Beattie halted the hack, and had to grab the edge of the footrest to keep his feet from flying out in front of him when his boots skated weightlessly across a hidden patch of ice.

Two matched footmen burst from the cottage with twin expressions of horror, but they were far too well-mannered to scold their guest for leaping down from a carriage like—what had Beattie said?—aye, like an overeager puppy.

Jonathan *liked* puppies. *Everyone* liked puppies. There were far worse things one could be compared to.

As the footmen carried Jonathan's trunks into the cottage—and really, only a duke could refer to this sprawling detached brick country home as a *cottage*—he turned back to Beattie to make his goodbye.

"Safe travels back to your wife." He tossed an extra sovereign up toward the perch. "I've left a small coin purse in the carriage for you to do with what you will. If it were me, I'd purchase a horse on my way out of town."

Beattie nearly missed catching the sovereign. "*How* much coin is in the back of my carriage?"

Jonathan waved a hand. "I didn't say you could purchase *'the'* horse. Perhaps I want the famous one for myself. I know nothing about horseflesh, but the best studhorse in England can't be a poor investment, can it?"

Beattie stared at him. "If they wouldn't sell it to Prinny—"

"Then he didn't offer the right price. I agree, I agree. You're a crafty one." Jonathan slapped the side of the carriage. "Go on now, before you beggar me dry."

As the wheels crunched over the snow, it almost sounded like Beattie muttered, "No one will believe this story."

Jonathan grinned to himself. All good stories were slightly unbelievable, and the *best* stories were the least believable of the lot. It was his sworn mission to live the unlikeliest tale he could devise.

"Mr. MacLean," said the duke's butler. "Allow me to take your hat and your coat. I'm afraid His Grace isn't expected until the day after tomorrow."

The duke's butler did *not* add, "Because you've arrived two days early."

Partly because a duke's butler was far too refined to make such a pointed observation, and partly because someone as well-prepared as Nottingvale would keep his cottage ready for guests at all moments, despite only hosting once per year during his annual Yuletide party.

"No, thank you," Jonathan said politely,

keeping his hat and coat. But he tipped the butler twice as much as the footmen all the same. "I've only just got here. I want to explore a bit before I settle in."

He would spend more than enough time in the duke's house once the others arrived. His partner, first. Jonathan had arranged the meeting, and Calvin was bringing all the illustrations and samples necessary for convincing the duke to invest in their sartorial venture. Jonathan had agreed to meet Calvin a day early to practice their proposal. Which meant, from tomorrow on, Jonathan would be stuck inside. This afternoon was his opportunity to explore the outside.

For such a small village to feel like an adventure, the key was to walk everywhere. It would take longer and he would notice more. Jonathan loved noticing things. He had learned to draw in order to remember all the things he noticed. He usually ended up giving those drawings away, aye, but that was because a vagabond explorer must travel light.

All Jonathan kept were memories.

He made exaggeratedly careful steps in the packed snow along the edge of the road. Sliding down a hill could be great fun when done on purpose, but twisting an ankle was no start for an adventure.

Also, he was wearing the smart traveling attire that Calvin had designed, with extra coat pockets and a cashmere-lined waistcoat. An impeccable carriage outfit, one which Jonathan could foresee being worn on countless future exciting journeys, so long as he didn't rip a hole in the knee flailing about on tricky hidden patches of ice between here and the castle.

Not that he was going *straight* to the castle. That was what ordinary people did when they visited Cressmouth on an ordinary holiday. The castle employed most of the town and housed most of its visitors. There could not be a more boring place to start.

Jonathan wanted to know who these people were that did *not* live or work in the castle. They couldn't all be dukes, and ducal servants. Some must be ordinary villagers, that couldn't be helped, but the same logic indicated some villagers must be *extra*ordinary, and those were the people Jonathan wanted to meet.

Cottage, cottage, cottage... He was friendly, aye, any gentleman ought to be, but not so pushy as to knock on the doors of complete strangers in the hopes of becoming momentary friends. The trick was to run across them casually, whilst they were walking down the street or riding an overpriced studhorse about their farm. Cottage, cottage...

What's this?

He jerked stock still, a posture that could have been mistaken for military precision were it not for the extremely flattering, extremely comfortable, only slightly wrinkled carriage outfit he wore as his uniform.

This was a shop of some kind, with the living

quarters upstairs, and a charming stone chimney with a faint plume of smoke.

From this angle, Jonathan couldn't make out the wooden sign swinging from squeaking hinges beside the door, but enough candles were lit inside to give the impression sunlight flowed out, rather than in through the many windows.

Open for business, then, and a perfect place to find something extraordinary.

Everything anyone could ever want was in the castle, Jonathan had been told. The rooms to let were a little dear, but the entertainment was free —musicians, dancing—as was the bountiful food. Three hot meals served daily in the grand dining chamber to anyone who wandered in, as well as refreshments just inside the castle doors for passers-by to enjoy. Mulled wine, hot chocolate, biscuits with and without raisins, no doubt. A lake, a hill, walking tours, an open-air market in the back garden, weather permitting. The list of delights went on and on.

But the castle couldn't have *everything*, no matter what they claimed. It wasn't a smithy, for one, nor was it a stud farm. Whatever this unassuming little shop contained, it was already *better* than the castle, because it had something the castle didn't.

Something Jonathan was about to discover.

He inched closer, careful not to slip on the ice and slide through the open door in an ungainly yet fashionable heap.

He almost fell anyway.

The shop contained the most stunning woman Jonathan had beheld in his life. Who cared what she was selling? He would be content to gaze upon her bonny face until the sun set and the candles sputtered out.

He could only see her from the elbows up due to some ill-thought-out wooden counter standing vexingly in the way, but her round, delicate shoulders were outshone only by the gentle brown curve of her neck, the stubborn angle of her chin, the lush softness of her lips—at least, Jonathan imagined them to be soft, but in this weather he would not hold a wee bit of chapped roughness against anyone. In any case, her nose was as lovely as her mouth. A little wide and a little snub; the perfect amount of roundness.

From this distance it was impossible to tell whether her eyes were the same dark brown as her skin or as black as the high chignon pinned so efficiently that not a single hair escaped. Could that be true? Or was he too far away to see past her perfection? He *liked* ruthless efficiency; it was a very fine quality, one he did not share at all. He also liked wild bits that escaped and did incorrigible things.

He supposed this meant that no matter how perfect or imperfect this woman was, she was destined to please him either way. Really, what sort of fool would pass up this opportunity to introduce himself? Jonathan was only here for a few days. Once Calvin arrived on the morrow, his time would be spoken for. If there was any hope of making this woman's acquaintance, the time was now. His blood raced enthusiastically at the prospect, filling his veins with energy and causing a delightful little flutter in his stomach.

Jonathan was on the cusp of another adventure. He could feel it.

CHAPTER 2

*M*iss Angelica Parker's quick, competent fingers secured the next amethyst in its delicate setting with deliberate, precise movements.

Everything Angelica did was deliberate and precise. The items on display in the front windows were at varying heights, depending on whether the intended wearer was a child or an adult. Because the fireplace was on the left side of her shop, comfortable chairs had been arranged on the right, with artfully placed hand mirrors atop each side table for admiring one's reflection.

The two-foot-wide counter that separated Angelica from the customers contained her primary work area on the left—the same side as the fireplace—and a curated display of higher priced items on the right—the same side as the customers. The most valuable jewelry was kept under lock and key, to be brought out from a private room by special request.

Every item in the shop was categorized and displayed just so. Every tool in her working area kept in perfect condition, waiting on its assigned hook or labeled drawer at exactly the right distance from where she'd be most likely to need it.

This winter, she was busier than was comfortable, but that was a good thing, a wonderful thing. She was blessed to have so much business. That her shop's seasonal success kept her from the large, loud, loving Parker family reunion taking place two hundred yards up the road was a disappointment she'd simply have to weather.

There would be time for family, *after*. Time for Christmas, *after*. Time for Angelica, *after*.

Matching necklaces for the Cruz sisters were to be completed today, followed by several other commissioned pieces that needed to be hung in stockings before Christmas came a fortnight from now.

Angelica longed for the comforting chaos of the Parker clan. A few took turns staying home to mind the family jewelry shop, but the rest came every year. Knowing so many family members were here in Cressmouth, having a marvelous time in a guest suite with a gorgeous view on the fourth floor of the castle, a stone's throw from her workshop, was both a comfort and torture.

Nothing rejuvenated her like her brother's booming laugh, the smiles and chatter of her nieces and nephews, her aunts' and cousins' diverting commentary about the food served in the dining area and the dances in the castle ballroom.

They were making merry, at least. That was the important part. If it was difficult to think so in this small, silent, empty shop without her family's laughter and noisy chatter surrounding her like a warm blanket, well, Angelica would simply have to keep going, like she always did.

As soon as she finished her work, she would join them. It might only be for an hour or two a night, but at least she would have them for a little while.

Perhaps this time when they returned home to London, they would be convinced of Angelica's talent and potential. They would understand why she had come here to Cressmouth, why it was worth it, what she'd accomplished. Perhaps this time, they would be proud of her.

The tinkle of the bell broke her concentration. She glanced up from the necklace to find a well-dressed gentleman in her doorway, his tall form and broad shoulders blocking the late-afternoon light.

Swiftly, she folded the black velvet over the necklace and its accoutrements, and pasted a welcoming smile onto her face.

"May I help you?"

"Mayhap," came a low, rich voice, with a droll undercurrent. "Probably not, to be honest, which is no reflection on you, but rather my own peculiarities."

Scottish? The burr was not as strong as some

she'd heard, but undeniably present. It felt like a tickle beneath her skin.

"But one never knows, does one?" he continued. "Walking through this door could spark the biggest adventure of my life. Which would say quite a lot, given the ones I've had so far. Or perhaps we've begun the greatest adventure of yours! Why hadn't I thought of that? Perhaps I'm to be *your* spark, rather than you mine. Shall we see?"

And with that, he stepped fully into the shop, flinging his arms wide into a dramatic pose as the door tinkled closed behind him.

Angelica did not say anything.

This was not an unusual occurrence. Her quiet reserve, that was, not this oddly compelling stranger. Angelica only felt comfortable when speaking about jewelry or when surrounded by family.

The stranger, however, seemed impossibly comfortable, maintaining both his expansive *voilà!* pose and an encouraging smile, as if he fully expected her to strike some complementary stance like two dancers at the start of a tragic opera.

"May I help you?" she said again, hoping the familiar words would turn this situation into something she knew how to deal with.

"I am Jonathan MacLean." He whipped his hat from his head and made an impressive leg. "At your service."

"I don't... require your services?"

Oh, why had the statement come out like a question? She did not rely on anyone but herself, and she'd never heard of Jonathan MacLean. He was not a person one was likely to forget.

He stepped further into her shop, which took him out of silhouette and cast his face into light.

Angelica's breath caught.

Could he tell that her silence was because he'd stolen her words?

She should not find a gregarious, presumptuous Scot this attractive. His eyes were a crystalline blue, his lips thin, his jaw strong, his cheekbones stolen from a statue, his skin the same moonstone pinkish-white as the lords and ladies who attended parties like the Duke of Nottingvale's.

And yet the sum of these features was greater than any one part. He was tall as a footman, broad-shouldered as a farmer, as winsome as Beau le Duc. His eyes glittered like sapphires of a thousand facets, above a bone-melting smile that had yet to falter despite her cool reception.

His dramatic entrance didn't make him look ridiculous at all, but heart-stoppingly magnetic. He seemed made for the stage, the sort of larger-than-life charisma and razor-sharp beauty that would draw crowds the likes of which Drury Lane had never seen. *Was* he an actor? Was he practicing a role, here, with her?

If so, she did not have time for it or him, no matter how unsettlingly handsome he was. There was no space in her life for distractions.

Especially tall, broad-shouldered distractions with eyes like jewels and a smile that melted knees.

"Ask me anything," he said. "Give it your best. Try to surprise me."

Angelica rolled back her shoulders. She had a question, all right. One he was refusing to answer.

"May I help you?" she said again, more pointedly this time, each syllable as sharp as his cheekbones.

He beamed at her as though she had passed a test.

"Very good." His burr was as rich as melted chocolate. "I was expecting 'Who are you?' or 'Why are you here?' or 'Where are you from?' All of which, I might add, have easier answers."

"This is Cressmouth," she found herself explaining. "Strangers are the least mysterious thing that blows into town. We wouldn't be a Christmas village without tourists."

Something flickered in his eyes. He turned from her, as if not wanting her to witness the smile slipping out of place.

He was just as attractive in profile. *More* so. Or perhaps the lack of dazzling smile allowed her to better see the rest of him. From this angle, he seemed less impossibly cheerful and more... Hmm. Brooding wasn't it. Not quite sad, not quite wistful. Determined, and a little self-deprecating. As though the show hadn't been for her benefit at all, but rather for his. An audience of one, and a script perhaps no one but him would understand.

Her cousins would laugh themselves into fits if they could see Angelica studying some dashing Scotsman as though he were an uncut diamond brought to her for appraisal.

We told you to find a man, they would say, *but not that one. Auntie has picked out just the gentleman for you, though your brother thinks you'd be better matched with—*

No. Shutting out their noisy, nosy opinions on how she should live her life was one of the principal reasons Angelica maintained a strict no-relatives-in-the-jewelry-shop policy.

Once she received the recognition she craved, then and only then would she entertain the notion of marrying a husband *of her own choosing,* thank you very much. She welcomed her family's home cooking, but not their ham-fisted attempts at matchmaking.

She did not need or want a man to make her life complete. Angelica was enough, all on her own. She would prove it.

She opened her mouth to politely enquire for the fourth time whether she could be of service—oh, how she wished she could be rude without causing risk to her livelihood!—when Mr. MacLean spun to face her.

"This is a jeweler's shop!" Obvious delight lit his eyes. "I adore jewelry."

She scowled at him before she remembered only to assume neutral expressions. Why the dickens had the man burst through the door if he did not know what kind of shop this was?

She crossed her arms over her chest in preparation for the next inevitable question.

"The owner—" he began.

Here it came. The assumption every single person without fail had made once they crossed the threshold and discovered her on the other side. No one saw beyond her bosom or the tiger's-eye brown of her skin.

"—and designer of all this beauty is standing right before me." He beamed at her. "It's true, isn't it? You created these pieces yourself?"

Her arms fell limply down to her sides. He hadn't assumed she was an employee? Or a servant? Or property? In England, it was no longer legal to sell or purchase new slaves, but plenty of the wealthy kept the ones they had. She stared at him. "But... I'm..."

"Breathtakingly bonny? I did notice. Horrid manners for you to bring it up yourself, one might add. Aye, you outshine all these jewels, but they sparkle in their own way. Like this set..."

He wandered away to gaze closer at a collection of brooches at the far corner of the counter.

She stared after him speechlessly.

Breathtakingly bonny, he'd said. And then turned away. As though his words had not been empty flirtatious banter, pretty words designed to weaken a woman's defenses, but a simple statement of fact.

He *assumed* this was her shop. A Black

woman. He'd assumed the pieces were *her* handiwork. Complimented them. Thought her talented. Believed her intricate creations to be far more remarkable and noteworthy than the fact that Angelica owned and designed them. Her chest filled with hope.

He made everything she'd worked for all these years seem *possible*.

Despite his claim to the contrary, Angelica was uncomfortably aware that she was the least eye-catching thing in the room.

All her time and energy was devoted to her shop. Which meant everything else in her life was as plain and simple as possible, so she needn't waste precious time dithering. The pale-pink day dress she wore was identical to six others in her wardrobe. She could grab any item without thinking and it would all match because she'd designed her living quarters to be as easy as possible. She saved her brain for things that mattered. Her shop was her world. Her looks should be irrelevant.

A maxim she'd repeated to herself for seven long years, only for today—today!—for it to finally feel true.

Angelica looked like a business owner. She looked like a jeweler. Like a skilled artisan. She looked like she belonged here, in this space. In the shop she'd carved out of blood, sweat, tears, and pure unadulterated stubbornness.

All by herself.

Mostly by herself. In any case, she was on her

own now. Independent and proud of it.

"Tell me about all the pieces," commanded the distractingly handsome Scotsman. "Start at the beginning. Which was the first one you made? The first one you sold? Why that one? When did you open the shop? Are most of your clients tourists? Who was the first customer? Are you charging enough for your work? Which stones are your favorites to work with? Is gold better than silver? How do you come up with such compelling designs?"

Angelica stared at him.

Usually she didn't know what to say, but he'd given her too *much* to respond to. Asked better questions in one minute than all her other customers combined.

She didn't have *time* to explain how she became a jeweler, what her first piece was, why a bejeweled vinaigrette bottle had been the first item she'd sold. Much less give the hours-long—months-long?—explanation of which materials she preferred for which purposes and why, and the mechanics behind each design. He would have to apprentice her for a year.

"Och aye, I like this one," he breathed, seemingly unperturbed by her lack of answers. "May I touch?"

She nodded jerkily. The piece was a deceptively simple pendant; an orb within an orb, the interior world turning independently of the delicate golden cage that bound it.

Even though Mr. MacLean had asked permission to touch, received permission, *wanted* to touch, he brought his knuckle ever so close to the side of the tiny globe-within-a-globe and did not make contact.

Angelica was two yards away and could feel that light presence as though his knuckle was not next to her gold pendant, but rather beside her cheek. Close enough to feel his warmth, yet not quite touching. Close enough to lean into, were she to dip her head. Close enough to smell, to taste.

But it was not her he was looking at with such fascination. It was not even the gold pendant. Already he had moved to the next sparkling object, and the next, and the next. At this rate, he would lay eyes on every piece faster than she would have been able to rattle off their names.

When he reached the final piece, he stood just across the counter from Angelica. He could reach out and not-quite-touch her the way he'd not-quite-touched her gold pendant.

The thought made her want to wrench open the wooden door behind her, fling herself into her private adjoining cottage, and shut the door tight behind her.

She wouldn't, of course. She couldn't. Her shop didn't close for hours, and she needed every scrap of success she could find.

"I'll take them," the Scot announced.

She blinked at him. "Take what?"

"Whichever ones you want to sell me," he replied, as though it was obvious. As though people wandered in off the street every day willing to pay exorbitant prices for expensive jewelry they didn't bother to pick out for themselves.

He hadn't even *asked* about cost.

"What would you do with fifteen hair combs?" she managed.

"Is that what you'd sell me?" He appeared delighted by this absurdity. "I'd wear them, all at once, just to say that I did, and then I'd give them away to fifteen ladies who could better appreciate their value."

She stared at his neatly trimmed golden brown hair, the color of well-polished amber. It didn't even graze his ears. "You couldn't *fit* fifteen clips in your hair."

He grinned at her. "But I would *try*, which is what would make it such a comical tale. Shall I purchase them, then? You can be my witness. I'll tell everyone I meet, 'If you don't believe me, there's a lovely jeweler up in Cressmouth who saw the whole thing. Her name is...'" He leaned forward expectantly.

Now he was definitely close enough to touch. If she lifted herself on her toes, she could brush noses with him. Their proximity was appallingly improper.

Yet she didn't pull away.

"Miss Parker," she said instead.

She *could* have said "Miss Angelica Parker." Her Christian name was no secret. Despite living in the shadow of a castle, the village of Cressmouth didn't stand much on pomp and propriety. Many of those who lived here year-round first-named each other as though they were cousins who had grown up together since birth.

It felt like that sometimes. At once cloying and protective. An entire village of big brothers and big sisters, full of unsolicited opinions and unconditional love. Their livelihoods might depend on tourists, but their loyalties were to one another.

Mr. MacLean was an outsider.

He would leave just as suddenly—and likely as dramatically—as he'd arrived. He did not need to know her given name.

"Miss Parker," he said, as though tasting the syllables and finding them unexpectedly delicious. "It suits you."

It did? What was that supposed to mean? That she looked like a Miss rather than a Mrs., or that she seemed like a Parker, whatever that was?

"'MacLean' suits *you*," she shot back.

His sapphire eyes widened. "Does it? What does that mean?"

She swallowed. *This* was why she didn't like to talk to people she didn't know or speak on subjects she didn't command. She was bound to say the wrong thing.

"Your burr," she mumbled, waving a hand without meeting his eyes. "You sound Scottish."

"I am Scottish," he agreed. "For better or for worse. Your accent, on the other hand, is poor indeed. You sound…"

She tensed.

"...*English*," he whispered, and gave an exaggerated shudder.

"I am English," she managed.

"Pity," he sighed. "All jewels have their flaws, don't they? That is, not yours, obviously; your pieces are exquisite, even the hair combs. I would not be at all ashamed to wear them, all at once or otherwise. But English, now, there's a challenge. A man must set limits. Although I admit I find you a delight."

He did?

Strangers tended to find Angelica prickly and taciturn, not a delight. Even not-so-strangers. Two aunts and a distant cousin had independently informed Angelica she'd be married by now if she hadn't the general demeanor of a startled hedgehog. Adorable, but untouchable.

Armor was smart. Armor kept her protected. Armor let her do her job... which had been woefully neglected ever since Lord Rakish McChatterbox swept into her shop like a knight prancing before his maiden.

She had no time for men or idle chatter. Even if his nonsense had managed to settle her nerves in much the same way the noise of her family reunions did. If she didn't have a rule of not working in front of a client, she rather suspected she'd finish the Cruz necklaces faster with Mr. MacLean prattling in the background than she would left alone to her own thoughts.

Nonetheless, there was no room in her life for

anything but work until she'd reached her goals. No exceptions, not even for handsome Scots.

"No offense meant," she began, then cleared her throat and started anew.

He was less than an arm's width from her, which should make it easy to be heard, yet her words had been little more than a squeak.

"No offense meant, sir, but if you aren't going to make a purchase, I must get back to work." Was that offensive? It was probably offensive. He looked baffled. "It's not you," she added quickly, although it was definitely him. "It's that I'm untenably busy. My relatives are here, and I can't see them until I've finished these pieces, which at this rate—"

What was wrong with her? Now she was babbling just like Mr. MacLean.

"Who said I wasn't going to buy the hair combs?" he asked. "I'll take the bracelets as well, if that helps. And the earrings. You can charge me double for taking so much of your time. I only meant to—"

The door tinkled open and Noelle Ward, Duchess of Silkridge, dashed inside.

"Angelica! There you are."

"Where else would I be?" Angelica muttered, acutely conscious that Mr. MacLean now knew her Christian name. "I'm always here."

"And a good thing, too. We're in dire need of your help."

"'We' the Duke and Duchess of Silkridge? Or 'we' the castle counting-house?"

This question likely made no sense to Mr. MacLean. Before marrying a duke, Noelle had spent her days high in the castle's tallest tower, overseeing the counting-house.

From the look on Mr. MacLean's face, he could sense a fascinating story and was dying to ask a hundred impertinent questions.

"'We' the entire village of Christmas," Noelle said dramatically, which likely pleased Mr. Mac-Lean just as much. "For the grand Yuletide ball, we're erecting a large yew tree in the ballroom, and we need you to help us decorate it."

Angelica raised her brows. "Why?"

"You're the most talented artist in Christmas. The adornments must be the most beautiful objects our guests have ever seen—"

"No, not why would you ask me to design the adornments," Angelica explained patiently. "Why would you put a tree indoors?"

"It's tradition."

Angelica shook her head. "I've never heard of it."

"A *new* tradition," Noelle admitted. "It's the first annual Marlowe Castle Yuletide Indoor Evergreen—yes, I know that's a mouthful; we're working on a better name—and it absolutely has royal precedence. Queen Charlotte first decorated a large yew tree with fruits and baubles fourteen years ago, at Queen's Lodge in Windsor. All the beau monde is thinking of doing it."

"So... the plan is to copy High Society?" Angelica said doubtfully.

"Exactly. What does our village stand for, if not for making perquisites associated with aristocrats available to the general public? The castle is open at all hours with every manner of entertainment... And now a tree!"

"And now a tree," Angelica repeated. Exactly what she needed. There was already not enough time to finish all her work and still see her family, not to mention she was expecting a visit from a friend... How was she supposed to do it all? It was impossible. "What do you need?"

"Mr. Thompson has authorized me to commission ten gold adornments." Noelle lowered her voice. "And if he hadn't, I would have paid for it myself. Charge whatever you like, Angelica. I want this to be worth it for you. This will change people's lives."

Mr. Thompson was the solicitor managing the castle trust. *Charge whatever you like* was a convincing argument.

"How will decorating an indoor tree change people's lives?" she asked instead.

"Not everyone in Cressmouth is in a position to reap the rewards of tourism. Until now! We have endless hills of evergreens. What could be a better souvenir than a tree from the village of Christmas? Mr. Thompson has signed a document granting all year-round residents the right to sell a generous quantity of evergreens from five percent of the castle woods, to be replanted every spring. Not everyone will take advantage, but those who wish to... *can.*"

It was a worthy cause. Angelica had no time to take on another project, but saying no would be admitting to weakness—and letting her neighbors down. The ball was held the Wednesday before Christmas, making it only five days hence. If she didn't already have so much else to do…

"If we can pull this off," Noelle continued, "which we *will*, with your help—everyone will know you were the one to design the golden holly sprigs with red-jeweled berries.'" She leaned forward and lowered her voice. "All the wealthy tourists will want to take home adornments of their own, designed by the same artist. *You*, Angelica! They'll brag to all their friends and your name will be on everyone's lips."

Angelica's name on everyone's lips.

This was what she wanted. What she had worked so hard for, and for so long. She wanted *recognition*. She wanted tourists to flock to her door not because she was the only jeweler for miles, but because she was the only jeweler they wished to do business with.

"Eve will put it on the front page of the *Cressmouth Gazette*," Noelle was saying.

The rest of her words sounded as though they were muffled by water. Cressmouth's population might be small, but the gazette reached thousands of homes outside the village. Everyone who visited subscribed, as did countless more who took their Yuletide holidays vicariously through the antics printed in the monthly broadsheet. It might be on a small scale, but Angelica's name would be known *nationwide*.

All she'd have to do was give up her chance to be with her family.

She straightened her spine. There would be more Christmases in the future. Angelica would have enough money to take the entire clan on holiday thrice in a year anywhere they wished.

"All right," she said. "Golden holly with jeweled berries. The most beautiful—and expensive—Yuletide adornments ever created."

Noelle squealed and clapped her hands together. "I'll pick them up for the grand ball on Tuesday. Thank you, thank you, thank you. This will be marvelous."

She dashed from the shop before Angelica could say another word.

The interior filled with silence.

Mr. MacLean arched a golden brow. "If you didn't have time to sell me a bucketful of hair combs..."

"I know," Angelica said. "*I know.*"

How was she meant to explain it to him?

She took a deep breath. "This may sound conceited, but I work hard because I know how talented I am. Seven years ago, I vowed to create a name for myself at any cost. This is part of that cost, *and* my chance. Once my designs are respected all over the land, I'll have earned the right to relax, to be proud of myself, to do as I please. But until that day... I have work to do."

She expected him to launch into a thousand

questions. Why the vow? What cost? Why seven years?

Instead, he surprised her by giving her an unsettlingly serious stare, followed by a short, decisive nod.

"I have no use for Christmas," he said slowly, "but I understand vows and ambition. I'll leave you to it."

He strode out of the exit just as abruptly as Noelle, pausing only to give Angelica a little bow before disappearing through the door and into the falling snow.

She stared after him for far too long before she remembered the half-finished necklace. Angelica tried to return to her task. There would be no eating or sleeping until the Cruz pieces were finished and delivered, and she was free to start on the adornments for the castle tree.

But the shop felt empty without Mr. MacLean in it. As though when he'd left, he'd taken all the air with him. It was just Angelica now, alone, with no sounds to accompany her but the pounding of her heart.

She wished he'd stayed.

She was glad he left.

How could she miss a total stranger? She couldn't. It was impossible. She would shove him from her mind. No more thoughts of Mr. MacLean until after Christmas.

By then, he would be long gone.

CHAPTER 3

$\mathcal{J}$onathan opened all three of his trunks and bent over their contents.

It was strange to possess so many items. When he entered his room and saw three large trunks sitting there, it felt like he'd walked into the wrong guest chamber.

Over time, he would become used to it. He had to. If all went according to plan, he'd spend the next year or more traversing Britain with trunks full of Calvin's creations, convincing haberdashers and other shopkeepers to become distributors for the fashionable new Fit for a Duke ready-made collection of men's apparel.

If Jonathan performed his role well, Fit for a Duke's affordable order-by-catalogue fashions would be ubiquitous in no time. Jonathan's name would be right there on the cover. He would no longer need to prove himself. His success would speak for itself.

He glanced at his pocket watch. Its alarm had

awoken him at half past eight, as it did every morning. There was no sense wasting daylight. He glanced outside just long enough to see the sun rising through the falling snow, and quickly allowed the curtain to close. There would be no further exploring until business matters were resolved.

Calvin would be here at any moment, likely with several new trunks of affordably priced high fashion, every bit as impressive as the last. Today, they were to polish their presentation for the Duke of Nottingvale, whose public endorsement —and private patronage—would ensure Fit for a Duke's resounding success.

Impatient to be on his way, Jonathan grabbed the topmost "elegant but casual" ensemble rather than ring for a maid or footman. Today he chose pantaloons with ankle stirrups, a deep red waist-coat and dark blue frock coat, which could be paired with several thick winter capes. All the items in these trunks had whimsical, pretentious titles, because they were Fit for a Duke pro-totypes.

Until the illustrated catalogue was in every household in England, Jonathan was meant to be a walking advertisement:

High quality, affordable price, no valet required! Look like Brummell without breaking the bank. Wedding? Special occasion? Hoping to stand up with a sweetheart at the next village assembly? Page 23 has just the thing to win her heart and her hand!

In record time, he was buttoned and coiffed

and darting out of his too-quiet guest chamber in search of distraction. Calvin's coach would arrive at any moment, but until then, he couldn't be expected to sit about alone.

Jonathan greeted the duke's matched footmen effusively.

"Horace! Morris! How did you sleep? I must compliment Nottingvale on his guest quarters. I have never slept on a softer mattress. I hope this morning finds you just as well as it does me. Have you broken your fast?"

Although there was little to employ them until His Grace's arrival, they could not be coaxed into lively conversation.

He *had* learnt that Morris and Horace were nephews of a local cattle farmer. This no doubt aided in the coveted "matching" aspect of their employment, although they were shorter than the towering footmen most aristocrats preferred to boast. The use of local lads spoke highly of His Grace. Jonathan would expect no less. Nottingvale had charmed him from their first meeting in London, many years ago.

Calvin had also impressed Jonathan from the first. The clothier was talented enough to take England by storm, but too reclusive to bother.

That was where Jonathan came in! He wasn't the least bit reclusive or reticent. The two of them on their own could make a proper go of things, with the Duke of Nottingvale as patron and namesake.

Beau Brummell would tumble from people's

brains at once, the moment they realized they could replicate such peacockery at a fraction of the cost—and without boring themselves to tears with a three-hour toilette.

Jonathan couldn't wait to begin.

"A friend of mine will arrive at any moment," he informed the footmen.

Morris and Horace exchanged a doubtful glance.

"Don't worry," he assured them. "You needn't do anything special, other than bring in his trunks. We're setting up for a meeting with Nottingvale. I think the yellow parlor has the best light, don't you? It's perfect lighting for painting, which is advantageous, since I'll have an armful of illustrations to color once Calvin arrives. Can you tell the maids not to disturb the artworks if they see them drying on every surface? Never mind, I'll tell them myself. Enid's tooth was bothering her yesterday, and I want to see if she's getting on better after that poultice."

"Mr. MacLean," Horace said, then hesitated.

"Your visitor..." Morris added, then stopped.

Jonathan leaned forward eagerly. This was the most they'd spoken all morning. He would triple today's vails for this alone. "Aye?"

"Your friend won't be arriving," Horace said in a rush. "Snow has fallen nonstop since nightfall, and the roads are impassible."

"Won't be *arriving?*"

"It's a snowstorm," Morris explained helpfully. "Ankle-high now, and knee-high by tomorrow.

Every village for miles will be snowbound for at least a week, if not two."

"A week?" Jonathan squeaked. "Maybe *two?*"

Stuck here? Without his business partner? Without the duke? Without a *purpose?*

"What about the party?" he said inanely.

Calvin had been horror-struck when the duke extended coveted invitations to them, but Jonathan had been conflicted. It combined three of his favorite things all at once: a new location, something to do, and new people to meet.

It also celebrated his least favorite thing: Christmas. He had planned to continue traveling instead.

"The party will start when the guests arrive," Horace said apologetically.

"Which won't be for a week, maybe two," Morris repeated, in case Jonathan had somehow forgotten this element of the nightmare that was Cressmouth.

Small towns were perfectly fine when one could leave them in the morning. But being stuck in a tiny, snowbound *Christmas* village, of all disasters...

Jonathan needed a distraction.

Having something to concentrate on, an objective that required all his focus, was the one thing that kept him from thinking about all the things he tried so hard to forget. The last person he wanted to be alone with was *himself.*

"I'm going out," he announced. "I need my hat and coat."

"But the snow..." said Horace.

"Pah," said Jonathan. "Since we've been standing here talking, two sleighs and five people in caps and muffs have gone past the window."

"They're locals," Morris explained. "We're used to the snow. You're..."

Jonathan glared down at his fashionable limbs. "Dressed like a paper doll."

Aye, he could see the problem. See it and discard it and carry on despite it.

All three of his traveling trunks overflowed with attire perfect for lounging about a ducal "cottage" or dancing attendance on pink-cheeked misses at assemblies, none of which he intended to do. Just because his boots were made for waltzing didn't mean he couldn't trudge through snow in them, too.

He was an explorer! An adventurer! He would find something to do if it killed him.

The footman returned. "Your overclothes, Mr. MacLean."

"Thank you, Horace."

Jonathan shrugged into his thick coat, tugged on his gloves, pulled on his hat, wrapped his woolen muffler about his neck three times. There. He was ready for anything.

He slipped an extra vail for their trouble to both footmen as well as Mr. Oswald, the butler, then set out into the frigid weather.

Winter didn't frighten him. He was born in Scotland, where winters were no balmier than in England. The best antidote to the cold was something warm—like pies, for example. This was the perfect opportunity to see if the bakery he'd visited the prior evening was open. They might be baking delectable bannocks and cakes regardless of a little snow.

It had indeed fallen to ankle-length, but the villagers had not been idle. The pavement had been cleared on both sides of the road, leaving an unobstructed walking path between the castle and most of the village. The snow on the road was packed down in long stretches on both sides, likely in part due to the horse-drawn sleighs carting villagers and tourists who preferred not to walk in the snow.

Both efforts appeared to cease at the entrance to the horse farm. There was nothing after that but endless miles of hills and snow and evergreens. The road out of town already looked dangerous and impassible. Horace and Morris were right.

Jonathan pulled down the brim of his hat to deflect the flurries of snowflakes caught in the wind, and headed into the bakery.

The smell of hot fresh bread nearly lifted him off his feet.

"Ho there," he called out jovially.

"Ho there," Mr. Bauer, the baker, called back. "Another cinnamon biscuit?"

Jonathan was so startled, he almost toppled out of his kid leather gloves and shiny fashionable boots.

Although he introduced himself to everyone,

there was little reason for others to remember him. Jonathan never returned to the same town twice, thereby skipping right past any anxiety about whether he was half as memorable as he tried to be.

"*Two* cinnamon biscuits," he replied, then changed his mind. "Two of every biscuit."

Mr. Bauer's eyes twinkled. "Are you certain you don't want three of each?"

"I'd take all the biscuits," Jonathan admitted, "but then what would everyone else eat?"

The baker pointed at his great oven. "Come back in a quarter hour and find out."

"Perhaps I will come back," Jonathan said, surprising himself more than the baker. Being recognized and remembered was just as nice as eating warm, steaming bannocks. He placed a pile of coins on the counter. Enough to cover all the biscuits, just in case the baker had been serious about selling them to Jonathan.

He moved aside as a family burst through the door, exchanging familiar greetings and updates on this sister or that dairy cow with the baker.

Each word struck like lightning through Jonathan's chest. It was not so much envy as a bone-deep longing, a white-hot yearning to be this familiar to someone else. To be known.

He did not want Cressmouth in specific—anywhere but here!—but part of him had always been searching for a place to belong.

"Now, where did that spatula go?" The baker's

fat, flour-coated fingers tapped an empty peg on the wall. "It should be up here in its little home..."

Jonathan's chest felt hollow. Home was a place that was incomplete without you, where someone would notice when you left, would wish you were still there so that home would feel complete for them, too.

But no one had ever looked for him with a quarter of the intensity as the baker searching for his missing spatula—or half as much delight when they stumbled across him.

"There it is!" Mr. Bauer boomed, depositing two fresh pies into the outstretched mittens of two rosy-cheeked bairns before placing the spatula back on its peg with a comforting little pat. "There you go, back where you belong, next to your brothers."

The children's mother turned to Jonathan with a smile. "Good morning. Are you here to celebrate Christmas, or here to stay?"

Neither.

Why would he live in a place people *left?* He already knew the pain of being used to someone and having them ripped away. Loving and losing his mother had been hard enough. The only way to escape such heartbreak was to avoid close ties at all costs.

"Passing through." He accepted two large parcels of biscuits from the baker, and handed one to the children's surprised mother. "Have a splendid day!"

He slipped out of the bakery door before they could shower him with festive cheer.

The delicious smell of biscuits permeated the cold air. He *could* take his prize to the Duke of Nottingvale's cottage and split them amongst the staff, but returning so soon after he set out felt like giving up.

Besides, Nottingvale's staff had a ducal kitchen at their disposal, as well as a castle with unlimited refreshments up the road. Since His Grace wouldn't arrive for days, they could nip out and indulge their sweet tooth whenever they pleased.

Miss Parker, on the other hand, was unlikely to leave her shop for something so frivolous as freshly baked shortbread. After accepting that new project yesterday, Jonathan wouldn't be surprised if she'd stayed up all night working.

If anyone deserved a few dozen biscuits, it was Angelica Parker.

Rather than sweeping in through the tinkling door as he'd done the day before, Jonathan eased it open carefully, lest he disturb her.

She was at the back, behind the long wooden counter, just as she had been the day before.

Indeed, if Jonathan hadn't been certain that an entire night had passed since he had last seen her, he might believe he had opened the door and accidentally walked into yesterday.

She was wearing the same pink dress as before, though the puffed sleeves now had no wrinkles. Her glossy black curls were in the same chignon, and not the tiniest hair was out of place. Her eyes looked less tired. Her mouth twisted in an adorable expression of concentration.

She looked how he imagined she had looked yesterday morning, hours before he had first walked through her door. As though yesterday were the "after" and today the "before."

Jonathan had never been so intrigued. He took a closer look around her shop. Yesterday, he had inspected every single one of her beautiful, intricate pieces. They—like bonny Miss Parker herself—had distracted him from what *wasn't* present. No artwork hung upon the bare walls. No hanging silk, no wallpaper, just plain wainscoting. The counter itself was free from adornment, the display case naught but plain shelves behind glass.

It was as if she felt no need for the typical decorative flourishes other people strove to add to their homes and workplaces, because the beauty of her creations spoke for itself.

Like her understated surroundings, Miss Parker needn't add ostrich feathers or other ostentatious touches to draw attention to herself. She was gorgeous and perfect just as she was.

He swallowed. She had granted him permission to touch her art, but he had not done so, because it was not her art he longed to touch. It was Miss Parker he wished to explore. The unwrinkled gown, the soft tendrils of her hair, the contours of her lips.

These were not thoughts he could allow himself to entertain. Not with her.

Due to the snowstorm, he wouldn't be going anywhere. Intimacy of any kind was far too terrifying to consider when he couldn't walk away.

"Here for your hair combs?" Miss Parker asked without looking up from her work.

"Aye," he said. "If you're willing to sell them today. I also brought you a few biscuits."

At this, she looked up, and her brown eyes widened at the size of his package. "Do I look like the sort of woman who would eat two dozen biscuits?"

He shifted his weight. "What's the right answer to that question?"

"The answer is yes." She held out her hands. "Give them to me."

He closed the space between them and placed the parcel on the counter with a grin. "These are actually three dozen biscuits, which means there will be some left over for me, too."

She opened a drawer and retrieved two small white plates and placed them beside the parcel. "What kind did you order?"

"All of them," he admitted.

At last, she rewarded him with a smile. "My favorite kind."

She placed a cinnamon biscuit, a raisin biscuit, and a square of shortbread on her plate. He did the same.

"I don't have much time," she warned him. "I don't have any time, actually."

"There is always time for biscuits," he assured her. "I've done extensive firsthand research into the matter, and have never found a situation that could not be improved by delectable, sweet biscuits fresh from the oven."

She licked the tip of her finger. "You make an excellent argument. Are you a barrister?"

"I am an itinerant ne'er-do-well." He lowered his voice. "It pays much better."

She smirked and took a bite of her biscuit.

Jonathan excelled at this kind of conversation. Amusing, frivolous, superficial. It was easy to be likable and charming when there was no risk of exposing one's true self.

She narrowed her eyes. "You're not using these biscuits to woo me, are you?"

He shook his head solemnly. "Confirmed bachelor, madam. My work takes me everywhere, which means no staying long enough to develop warm feelings."

She arched a brow with obvious skepticism. "Heartless cad, are you?"

He nodded.

"So heartless, you brought three dozen biscuits to me for no reason, and gave away an equal amount?"

"Er," he said. "How did you..."

"The bakery is just across the street. I saw Mrs. Griffiths step outside with the package. She did not appear to have expected your gift."

"It wasn't for her. It was for the children. They were suffering a biscuit deficiency."

"Mm-hm." She moved her empty plate aside and cleaned her hands with a pitcher and towel. "You may go. Leave the biscuits."

He didn't move.

She sighed. "All right. Take the biscuits, if you must."

"I have nowhere to go," he admitted. "I'm used to constant motion, to being busy. Instead, I'm... here."

"Cressmouth has loads of things to do," she said in surprise. "Haven't you seen the gazette? No less than two entire pages of broadsheet are dedicated to all the Yuletide activities throughout the village. For example, there's—"

"I don't want any of that," he interrupted. "Perhaps I should try to live like a local, rather than a tourist. That would be a wee adventure, wouldn't it? A funny story to tell new acquaintances later. 'Have you been to Cressmouth?' they'll ask. 'The castle, the winter play, the snowy panorama, all the Christmastide activities?' And I'll say, 'Pah to all that. I lived like a local!'"

She held up a loupe, inspecting him through one magnified eye as though he were a strange specimen. Her eye looked large and lovely. He wanted to paint it.

"Have you ever lived like a local anywhere?"

"Not in years," he replied cheerfully. "I don't even remember what it means. Do locals eat lots of biscuits? I'm good at that. I suppose I could find a temporary post. Are you in the market for an apprentice?"

"No," she said flatly.

"I can pay you," he said. "I have money."

She crossed her arms. "I do not have time to train tourists. I'm after something bigger than money."

Now that was interesting. He leaned closer. "What *do* you want?"

CHAPTER 4

What did Angelica want?

A simple question that ought to have an equally simple answer. She wanted to be left alone so she could finish her work.

But *did* she want him to leave?

He had brought her biscuits, which ought not to be a deciding factor in an adult woman's decisions—and if not, surely spoke more to Angelica's addiction to cakes, rather than any warm feelings toward Mr. MacLean specifically.

Thoughts of her endless lists of tasks had woken her at dawn, and she had thrown herself into her work without bothering to break her fast. It was now half ten, and Mr. MacLean had likely saved her from fainting.

That was surely the reason her knees had felt strangely weak when he entered the shop.

"I..." she said.

He leaned closer.

She wished he wouldn't.

From this distance, she could see striations of dark blue lapis lazuli in his sapphire irises. His eyelashes were thick, the golden-brown shade found on the underside of shortbread. He did not smell of soap, but sweet biscuits and fresh bread. A warm, cozy scent that made her wish to bury herself within it; to wrap the scent around her and snuggle in close.

Mr. MacLean was as tempting as any treat she had ever sampled, but Angelica had no time to indulge even the tiniest nibble.

"I need to concentrate," she said firmly. Or would have said firmly, if her voice hadn't decided to crack and come out a breathy whisper. She cleared her throat and tried again. "The Yuletide ball is in four days. If they write about me in the *Gazette*..."

"It's important?"

"The most important thing to happen since my shop opened. It's the opportunity I've been waiting for. It's just been difficult to concentrate." She nudged one of the pieces on her work board. "I normally spend the Yuletide with my relatives. It sounds odd, but I think best when I'm surrounded by their noise. I've been at this tiara since dawn, but my shop is so... empty. The silence weighs on me."

"Ah." He nodded slowly. "I understand wanting to escape loneliness. I don't even have a home, which means every time I go somewhere, I must start from the beginning. It hadn't occurred to me that someone with roots might feel the same way."

"No." She looked at him sharply. He hadn't understood at all. "I'm not like you. I have a home. I don't have to begin anything again. My family is inside that castle. I can see it from here. Even if they weren't close by, I have other friends. There's no reason to be lonely. I'm *not* lonely."

Her family had predicted she would be. London was home to a million people, ten or twenty thousand of whom were Black like the Parkers. And Angelica intended to move to a village of one or two thousand total inhabitants? Was she *daft*? How would she find a husband up there?

But she wasn't daft. She was *ambitious*. And she wasn't the least bit interested in finding a husband. If her time was limited now as an independent woman, how much harder would it be to achieve her aspirations if being some man's obedient wife came first?

Besides, Cressmouth was small, but it wasn't the surface of the moon. More tourists flocked in this street every winter than had ever passed by her father's shop in Spitalfields.

When it wasn't Christmastide, the villagers formed their own big family. The Black community here was smaller, but no less loving. Her neighbors were friendly, all the shopkeepers looked after one another, and she never missed a church service. Angelica belonged here. If she weren't overwhelmed with work, she'd be over-whelmed with dinner parties and seasonal invitations.

She wasn't *lonely*. She was industrious.

It was not at all the same thing.

"I'm just busy," she said. "That's all." She made a big show of resuming her work on an emerald tiara for one of her customers. "If I had time for people, I'd be with my relatives. But I cannot leave my shop until all the work is complete. People rely on me. *I* rely on me."

"Just to make certain I understand," Mr. Mac-Lean said politely. "You miss your family. Their noise makes you happy. You can't leave your shop. Your relatives are in the castle."

She glanced up from the tiara to glare at him.

He gave her a brilliant smile. "Why not invite them here?"

"My goodness, that thought has never occurred to me," she said in a tone dripping with so much sarcasm it could wipe the shine off his boots.

Yes, their chaos rejuvenated her... in carefully regulated circumstances.

If she allowed any of them in, her brother would insist on taking control. He had his own, bigger shop in London. He'd be judging her the entire time. She wasn't ready for that yet.

The family noise and chaos revitalized her when it was somewhere *else*. When it was around her, but not about her. When the topic was Christmastide.

"What if," said Mr. MacLean, "the trick is not to run yourself ragged but rather to take a small respite now and then?"

"I took a respite," she reminded him. "I ate three biscuits."

"A large respite," he amended. "Gargantuan, by your standards. A period of rest that involves stepping outside of your shop, for an hour or two. It might invigorate you more than you think."

She shook her head. "I don't deserve a rest yet. There will be time for that once the adornments are hung and my name is in the *Gazette*. Until then, I have work to do and a shop to make presentable—"

"Make... presentable?" He gazed about the interior, then fixed wide eyes back on her. "What's left to do? Alphabetize the three dust motes that followed me in?"

She crossed her arms. "There is nothing wrong with keeping things generally neat."

"If this is 'generally neat,' I'd hate to see what your idea of 'obsessively ordered' might be." He grinned at her. "I'd better not invite you to see the utter destruction in my guest chamber."

"Who says I'd want to be anywhere near your —Wait, aren't you staying at the Duke of Nottingvale's cottage?"

"Previously known as a ducal cottage, aye. Now known as Utter Destruction."

She laughed despite herself. "He would never allow that to happen."

"He's not here," Mr. MacLean said cheerfully. "I've given all his servants permission to run amok."

"Let me guess," she said. "That's why you're here buying biscuits for me. None of Nottingvale's staff would leave their posts for a minute."

"Not even for a second," he agreed sorrowfully. "Not even to play *marbles*."

"Might I ask how an 'itinerant ne'er-do-well' managed one of the most sought-after invitations of the season?"

"That is an appallingly impertinent question," Mr. MacLean informed her, "which means it's my favorite kind. You can ask me anything, at any time. I'm an open book." He affected a grand pose. "His Grace and I are collaborating on a textiles venture. Or we will be, once he and my business partner arrive, and we're able to impress and astonish him with the merits of our proposal."

"His Grace will be investing in textiles?" Angelica said in disbelief.

"Finished ones," Mr. MacLean clarified. "Stylish apparel for the not-particularly-discerning man who wants to *look* like the pinnacle of taste and fashion. Calvin wanted to call it Dandy-in-a-Box, but I talked him into Fit For a Duke. We're selling the feeling of being indistinguishable from one's betters without fussing with valets and tailors. One needn't *know* fashion plates to look like one. All at affordable prices, as easy as picking a favorite picture from a catalogue."

"That's... clever," she admitted. "If you launch Fit For a Duchess, I would probably order a gown or two."

"No, you wouldn't. Your entire wardrobe is full of exact copies of one item."

"Why would... How did you..."

"It's my job to be observant," he explained. "I travel about, looking for the most profitable opportunities, and then I exploit them. For example, I—What is it? Why are you looking at me like that?"

"Oh, I don't know," she said tightly. "'Travel,' 'exploit', 'most profitable.' I suppose you're involved in slavery."

"I am not," he said, aghast. "Trafficking slaves is technically illegal on British soil and *ought* to be fully illegal throughout the Empire and everywhere. Hell is not good enough for men who believe themselves gods over others. The only business ventures that interest me are those that *provide* opportunities, not conscienceless schemes to take opportunities away. I want to lift people up, not keep them down."

Angelica stared back at him without speaking. Even with the slave trade becoming illegal on English soil seven years ago, it had not stopped many aristocrats and wealthy land owners from maintaining ownership of existing slaves. In fact, many increased efforts overseas, where there were not so many laws to impede turning a tidy profit.

Some men who did not dabble in slavery did

not refrain by choice. They lacked the funds to purchase a ship of terrified human beings, or the connections to build a plantation.

Mr. MacLean claimed to be morally opposed to the horrid practice on all counts. In his case, Angelica found she believed him.

He had treated her from the very first as though neither her gender nor her color had any bearing on what sort of person or how talented a jeweler she might be.

She was relieved Mr. MacLean championed abolition. He was a stranger, a tourist; yet a growing part of her hoped he would keep coming around.

She concentrated on setting emeralds so he could not see her face. "Is this your first business venture?"

"My hundredth," he replied.

Skeptical, she lifted her eye from her loupe.

"Not all ventures are successful. My first several were dreadful failures, yet some of the most important things I've ever attempted, because I learned from them. For years now, every partnership has been profitable. At different levels, of course. One cannot expect the same percentages from a mullioned window factory as a lemon-ice cart. The principle is the important thing."

"You invested in a *lemon-ice cart?*"

"No," he said. "I invest in talent. Calvin is the most brilliant clothier I have ever known, and it will be my privilege to help him bring his designs to those who would not otherwise have access.

On my travels, I have met talented sculptors, philosophers, inventors, professors, architects. If the only thing standing between them and success was a few pounds here or there and a wee bit of advertising, well, that's where I come in. What good is a logical mind or piles of coin unless one puts them to good use?"

"You don't just invest in people," she said slowly. "You invest in *ordinary* people."

He nodded. "Why invest in the firstborn son of a wealthy nobleman? He's already got every advantage life has to offer, and probably no good ideas to show for it. Whereas there are a thousand brilliant notions a day—perhaps millions, who knows?—that are thought and forgot because the people who had them could not act on them."

"That's... very sweet."

"It's not sweet," he said quickly. "It's self-serving and lucrative. Every person I help to succeed, helps me to fatten my bank account. I'm not funding charities, Miss Parker. I'm providing capital in exchange for healthy interest rates. I make money using other people's genius."

"It's still sweet," she said airily, since for some reason the thought rankled him. "It's as if you have the Christmas spirit year-round."

"I *do not*," he said in a huff. "I have self-advancing financial acumen year-round."

"Mm-hm," she said. "A selfish egotist who creates opportunities for the less fortunate. Have you seen my porcelain palette?"

"Listen to me," he said as he passed her the palette. "My dealings have nothing to do with Christmas and everything to do with simple mathematics."

"Is anything ever simple?" she asked.

"Some things are." He fixed her with his sapphire eyes. "Let's make an arrangement."

"I don't want your money," she said quickly. She *did* think his investment stratagems sweet, but Angelica would make her way on her own.

"So you mentioned." His tone was bemused, as though he was not quite certain what to make of her. "We've also established that you are overworked, and that I am an adventurer in want of an adventure. I know little about this village—"

"I do *not* have time to play tour guide to tourists. There's a guided walk about the castle grounds on Saturday afternoons."

"—and I'm uninterested in doing what everyone else does." His low burr warmed her skin. "The thought of living like a local until my business partners arrive amuses me, but I've no idea where to begin. Here's the agreement. You help me assimilate and I'll be your footman."

"You'll be my *what?*"

"Your servant; your errand boy. I'll fetch your food, provide aural accompaniment—"

"Are you *certain* you're skilled at making advantageous business arrangements?"

"I adore doing new things and meeting new people. What is boring and commonplace to you will be new and interesting to me. I've also never been a footman before, and I find the idea quite tickles me. I'm inordinately fond of improbable travel stories, and this arrangement has all the makings of a classic."

"You're speaking as if we've already agreed. What makes you think I'd want your 'aural accompaniment?'"

"You told me yourself: loud chaos relaxes and revitalizes you. As it happens, 'loud' and 'chaos' are my top two talents."

"I said my *family's* loud chaos would be welcome. You are not family."

"You said your relatives aren't allowed to cross the threshold. I am, and I haven't shut up yet. Clearly, it's helping. You finished your tiara."

"I'm—" She stared down at her work board.

It *was* finished. She'd moved on to the matching earrings without registering. His voice and his stories were every bit as relaxing as the comforting noise of her family, but without the accompanying anxiety.

"All right," she said slowly. "We can try it. Just until the duke arrives or I finish my work, whichever comes first."

He grinned at her. "Agreed. What time should I bring dinner, and do you prefer red or white wine?"

"Just to make sure we understand each other," she said firmly. "This is a ridiculous business arrangement, not a romance. I won't entertain sins of the flesh until I'm married—"

"At which point it won't be sins of the flesh," he said helpfully. "It'll just be pleasurable."

"—and I'm uninterested in attracting a suitor," she finished.

"I've no intention of suiting," he said solemnly, "so we are very well matched indeed. I simply wish to explore my present surroundings as though I'll never see them again, because that is, in fact, the plan."

His easy agreement with her conditions should not cause a sharp little twist in her belly, but there it was.

"I'm to send you on any and every mission I can think of, no matter how menial?"

"I've no pride whatsoever," he assured her. "I'm just looking for a good tale to tell one day."

"In that case, Mr. Footman, go and find the castle solicitor, and ask to work with the road-cleaning volunteers *and* the pavement-sweeping volunteers. If you've any time left, there's a bucket, a scrubbing brush, and vinegar and soap under the counter, which can be used to brighten the front windows of my shop, so that passers-by can see the items on display. And if you need even more adventure, there's always wood to be chopped."

Rather than balk at such a preposterous list of demands, he nodded as if committing each word to memory.

"Solicitor, snow duty, then bring you some wood. Your wish is my command." He beamed at her. "Shall I also don a powdered wig?"

"Do not put on a powdered wig."

"I'll find a marvelous one," he assured her. "You'll love it."

"I will not—"

But he was already through the door and gone, hurrying off to do her bidding.

CHAPTER 5

At ten o'clock the next morning, Jonathan made his way uphill despite the wind chapping his cheeks and the snow clinging to his lashes.

Winter had been pummeling him since dawn, but the road was clear from horse farm to castle, the pavements were swept, and a fresh bale of firewood had been piled on the stack behind Miss Parker's shop.

He had wanted to impress her, but wasn't certain how. She was not swayed by his offers to purchase anything—or everything—in the shop. She would rather sell her hair combs one by one to women who wanted them than to have Jonathan purchase the lot just because he could.

No one had ever declined his money before.

He'd expected nominating himself as her temporary footman to be a lark. He hadn't expected feeling so… *useful.* It was typically not Jonathan, but rather Jonathan's bank account that made people happy. It was a thousand times more satisfying to be the reason himself.

If yesterday was any indication, Miss Parker would have forgotten to break her fast this morning, and would be too stubborn to pause for sustenance.

Jonathan would pause for her. Now that he'd completed his early morning footman duties, he had all the time in the world. Who better to spend it with than someone who wouldn't take time for herself?

He stomped the snow from his boots beneath Marlowe Castle's protective stone archway and swept in through the great open doors.

Warmth enveloped him. Heat and noise, and the smell of cake and hot chocolate from the buffet just inside the entryway. He tried to determine which sensory pleasure was most welcome and decided Miss Parker was right: noise was the best. Crackling fires were a godsend, and pies were lovely at any hour, but the noise of *people* meant one needn't enjoy them alone.

That was the best part about spending one's life flitting from place to place: all the new people to meet. The second-best part was that if things didn't work out, it didn't matter. He was leaving anyway. There were endless chances to try again.

He helped himself to a biscuit at the refreshment table, taking care to introduce himself to all the other guests milling about Marlowe Castle's large reception room.

When Jonathan was a child, the thought of introducing himself to a stranger had nauseated him. Rarely could he mumble out *MacLean* without his skin flaming fiery red and his stomach doing somersaults. But he had tired of feeling like he didn't belong. Especially when he knew he wouldn't be staying. Jonathan didn't enjoy feeling awkward in strange places, so one day he'd decided to pretend *not* to anymore. He would become like a slate of roofing tile: anything he didn't wish to hold onto slid right off of him. Now the trick was second nature.

Once he made the acquaintance of two dozen guests, a half-dozen villagers, and a veritable army of castle staff, he followed directions across the great hall and up the winding marble stairs to the castle's ample circulating library. Its contents were free to the public, and Jonathan had been promised the well-stocked shelves contained topics for everyone.

He hoped that included something for Miss Parker.

Although Jonathan never stayed anywhere long enough for the purchase of a subscription to a local lending library to make financial sense, his first act in many places was to join as many libraries as possible anyway. The communal reading rooms were an excellent place to meet new people and get information that might not be found in the pages of a guidebook.

To his surprise, the castle's library was not only vast, but unguarded. Rather than a separate reading room, comfortable sofas and chairs were scattered throughout, and the books were *right there* for anyone to pick up and leaf through.

It was so lovely, he wished he could pay tenfold for the experience, and was bitterly disappointed such a delight was being forced upon him for free. There wasn't even a counter upon which one might surreptitiously leave behind a small stack of sovereigns.

There was, however, a black cat eyeing him with suspicion.

"Why, good day, sir," he said to the cat.

It arched its spine, black fur spiking as sharp claws extended from its front paws.

A young woman stepped out from what might have once been a reading room, and was now an extension of the library.

"Your Grace," she said.

Jonathan bowed. "A plain mister, I'm afraid. Jonathan MacLean, at your service."

"Not you." She pointed to the cat. "That's Duke. He's not a sir."

"I see." Jonathan did not see. He made a fine leg for the cat anyway. "Pardon my insolence, Your Grace."

The cat hissed its displeasure, then retracted his claws and sauntered away.

Jonathan hoped it wasn't an omen for his upcoming meeting with Nottingvale.

The young woman was still staring at Jonathan's cravat with about the same amount of suspicion as her cat.

"Er," he said brightly. "Is there a custodian or librarian?"

"No," she answered, and tilted her head. "But we've the latest Minerva Press Gothic novel on the third shelf in the second cubbyhole to your right."

"Oh, no," he said with a little laugh. "It's not for me. I—" He blinked. "Did you say, the latest Minerva Press novel?"

He had been obsessed with the genre ever since he'd stumbled across *The Mysterious Hand*, in which the hapless protagonists faced a handsome yet diabolical villain who was at once an inventor, an athlete, and a poet—and definitely not to be trusted when confined together in a hot air balloon.

But how had this woman known Jonathan delighted in Gothic drama? Did her cat smell it on him and give her a secret sign?

"It's not for me," he said again. "It's for Miss Parker, the—"

The young lady spun on her heels without explanation, selected what appeared to be three random books from shelves on three different walls, and placed the leather-bound stack in Jonathan's hands.

"—jeweler." He tried to figure out what was happening. "Since she won't rest, I thought I'd take the respite to her, in the form of a book. Like these. In my hands."

The young woman was not interested in his explanation. Before he'd finished speaking, she had already turned and disappeared into an adjoining room.

"Very well, then," Jonathan muttered. "We'll start with these three and see how it goes."

He read the titles of the books in his hands. One appeared to be religious parables of some sort, another was a compendium of songs and dance music by Ignatius Sancho, and the third a geologist's *Field Guide to Igneous, Sedimentary, and Metamorphic Rock.*

Not *precisely* the topics a fiction-lover like Jonathan might have chosen, but if the not-a-librarian had scented his love of Gothic horror without any hints, perhaps her divination skills would be just as accurate for Miss Parker.

He tucked the volumes into his leather satchel, left a small pile of coins in the newly created blank spaces on each of the three shelves, then made his way down the marble stairs to the castle's great dining hall.

Jonathan wasn't just going to deliver books. He was also going to deliver Miss Parker her luncheon.

Much like the circulating library, Marlowe Castle's busy kitchens offered free hot meals to local visitors and tourists alike, whether or not they were renting one of the many guest-chambers upstairs.

Although the hour was too late for breakfast and too early for dinner, many of the tables were full of smiling, chatting patrons, some enjoying all manner of sumptuous refreshments, and others clearly hoping to encounter neighbors, without contending with the spitting snow and blustering wind.

Jonathan very much approved.

He introduced himself to anyone whose eyes met his as he passed, and was delighted by the number of locals who invited him to share a meal or a bit of conversation.

"Next time," he said, surprised to discover he hoped it was true. He forced himself to continue on until he found a member of the staff who might pack a meal for two.

Despite the impressive menu, the moment the words "Miss Parker" had left Jonathan's lips, the staff had known immediately what should go in the parcel. Apparently, when she wasn't impossibly busy, Miss Parker took many of her meals here in the castle. In fact, according to one of the maids cleaning tables, it was unusual indeed for Miss Parker not to be present when her family was here for Yuletide.

Family. Jonathan didn't know if he loved or hated that word.

So as not to analyze it overmuch, he changed the topic at once, and applied himself to attempting to pay for his meals. When the staff could not be bent on this score, Jonathan settled for tipping each of them extra vails for their trouble.

"Are you off to Miss Parker's now?" asked a ruddy-cheeked maid with white curls.

"Aye," answered Jonathan, then changed his

mind. "I may pick up a few biscuits from the bakery on the way."

"Ah," said the maid. "See how Stephen's foot is getting along."

"Is Stephen the baker?" Jonathan asked.

The maid laughed. "Hardly. Stephen's his eight-year-old son. Sledded his foot into a tree yesterday, trying to race his brothers. Lads that age have bottomless stomachs. I'd wager he's eating the best buns as fast as Mr. Bauer takes them out of the oven." She flicked her fingers. "Off with you then, before the food goes cold."

Unsettled by the brief conversation with the maid, Jonathan closed the distance between the castle and the bakery slower than his usual jaunty pace. Although he'd mastered the art of introducing himself to others, he had failed to give much importance to their replies.

Jonathan had introduced himself to the baker, but hadn't considered the person Mr. Bauer was outside of the bakery. Jonathan might have heard everyone in Scotland's thoughts on the war, the weather, and the Prince Regent, but he didn't know *them*.

He kept all conversations superficial. Eighty percent commentary on the weather, ten percent complaints about traffic, five percent directions to the next town, and the rest signing his name in guest books when he checked into the next inn or posting house on his route. It was easy to be charming when one didn't expose one's true self.

He'd always thought he liked it that way. Cleaner. Easier. Now he wasn't so certain.

Perhaps a small change of plans was due.

He pushed open the door to the bakery.

"Ho there, Mr. MacLean," the baker called out. "More shortbread, is it?"

No, not "the baker." *Mr. Bauer.* Who had been paying more attention to Jonathan than Jonathan had to him.

His neck heated.

"Shortbread for me," he agreed, "and whatever Miss Parker would like best. How is Stephen's foot?"

The baker's face lit up. "Only thing wounded on that boy is his pride. Can't admit to losing a race to his younger brother, can he? But I play along, and let him eat all the hot buns he likes." Mr. Bauer chuckled and handed Jonathan a paper parcel. "Go on, then. Miss Parker must be waiting for you."

Jonathan left a pile of coins on a corner of the counter and headed toward Miss Parker's shop.

He'd bothered to learn *her* name, hadn't he? But he didn't know much more than that. He would have made a muck out of choosing the right library book for her, if Cat Lady hadn't been there to save him. And he wouldn't have known Miss Parker's first name was Angelica, if he hadn't overheard one of her actual friends use her Christian name. She didn't *want* him to know. Jonathan was a stranger.

He could do more. He could *be* more.

Connecting on a level slightly deeper than the superficial didn't terrify him *at all.*

Jonathan liked Miss Parker more than he wished to admit. Liking someone too much led to pain when he inevitably lost them. He must take care only to like, and never to love.

Miss Parker was dangerous. He liked her because he didn't have to *try* to like her. She was witty and bonny and clever. Liking her was easy and uncomplicated.

At least, it *had* been uncomplicated. Strangers' opinions couldn't hurt him. This new plan of truly coming to know someone else—of letting them stop being a stranger—risked someone else truly coming to know *him.*

Although it would only be for a week or two, the prospect made him feel disturbingly vulnerable. What if he tried to make real friends with her, and couldn't? What if it worked beyond his wildest dreams, only for him to have to walk away?

Which one was worse?

CHAPTER 6

*A*ngelica felt Mr. MacLean's proximity long before the bell tinkled above her shop door.

She'd looked up from her swage at the exact moment he'd stepped into view, whistling his way down from the castle before vanishing into the bakery across the street. She also happened to glance up once again the moment he'd stepped out of the bakery.

Or maybe her gaze had been on the front window all along instead of concentrating on her work.

As he entered, Mr. MacLean flashed a smile she could feel all the way to her toes. He lifted a pair of delicious-smelling parcels. "I brought you a present!"

Her stomach growled in response.

Angelica ignored her stomach. And the tingling in her toes. She might take whatever was in those parcels off his hands, but Mr. MacLean she ought to send packing.

"I said we could have *dinners* together." She cast her gaze pointedly at the clock behind her. "It's not dinnertime."

"And yet, one must eat." He placed the parcels in the middle of the counter, between her work area and the display of jewelry.

"One must do one's work," she corrected, but it was no use. Her belly's insistent grumbles loudly drowned out her own.

In her haste to return to her work, she'd once again failed to break her fast this morning. The Yuletide ball was in two days.

"One small respite," she informed Mr. Mac-Lean, who grinned at her. "One very quick, very fast, minuscule—*ow*." A flash of heat slashed through the muscles of her wrist, convulsing the muscles of her hand. The tools she'd been at-tempting to carefully put away clattered into the drawer.

In seconds, Mr. MacLean was there in front of her.

"Let me see," he demanded.

She rotated her wrist carefully, wincing at the pain. "It's nothing."

"It's something," he said firmly. His eyes were not on her wrist, but rather on her face. His rakish smile was gone.

She shook her head. "It happens all the time."

He raised a brow. "*All* the time?"

Well... all the time when she worked too much

for too long without pause. Sometimes she held tiny tools in a cramped position for hours on end. Her muscles forgot what it was like to finally let go.

Mr. MacLean held out his hand, palm up. "May I?"

She wasn't certain it was wise.

She was a Black woman with no husband. A professional jeweler in her place of business.

Mr. MacLean was not her friend. He wasn't even a customer. He was a foppish white man who'd entered her shop on a lark because he was bored, and had nothing better to do with his time.

But he'd asked permission. And the secret truth was... Angelica was desperate to know how it would feel if he touched her.

Not "if." *When* he touched her.

She gave a little nod and held her crooked wrist out, just above his palm. She would not place her hand in his. He would have to do it himself.

His hands were warm and impossibly gentle. Strong and firm, as confident as the man himself. Smooth, as though he'd never worked a day in his life.

The pad of his thumb feathered softly against the inside of her wrist.

Her fingers flexed involuntarily, but not in pain. At the shock of her hand cradled in his, at the pleasure of being caressed so tenderly.

Everything about her hand felt suddenly unfamiliar. The way her muscles melted at the slow, calming strokes of his thumb. Over long, patient minutes, he coaxed all the tension from her wrist, then the base of her palm, then the center, tracing each line again and again before moving to the pads below her fingers and thumb, then the fingers themselves, one by one, gently, deliciously.

If it weren't for the sturdy wooden counter between them, Angelica herself would have melted right into his exquisitely tailored chest.

Pity he was leaving after Christmas. She would pay him to stand here for the rest of their lives, her hand in his, massaging away all the pain until all she felt was this soporific lightness, as though the world weren't quite real, and all that existed was the warm stroke of his thumb against her sensitive flesh.

She could kiss him for this. The thought made her lift her languorous gaze from her utterly relaxed fingers to the sharp angles of his jaw, his firm, narrow lips. Angelica did not lift her gaze higher. She didn't want to see him watching her drink him in.

Mr. MacLean was handsome as sin, blast the man. He knew it, of course. It was in every stitch of his clothing, the swagger in his stride, the way his impish grin lit him from the inside whenever her eyes met his.

Even though her tendons had long given up their tremors, his talented fingers continued their sensual onslaught, as though he had been put on this earth to bring her pleasure.

No touch had ever been so relaxing and so intimate at the same time.

It terrified her.

"Thank you," she managed. "We should... I should..."

He didn't let go.

She didn't pull away.

Thank the Lord there was two feet of solid oak counter between them.

"The food," she whispered. "It'll go cold."

He set down her hand as though it was the most precious thing he had ever held, and then turned toward the parcels.

While he wasn't looking, she pressed her sensitized palm to her thundering chest. Angelica wondered if she would ever be able to pick up a jeweler's tool again without thinking of Mr. MacLean and this moment.

She may have sent him on a foolish mission to prove he was a fish out of water, yet it was he who made her feel as though she were coming up for air for the first time.

"Do you want me to leave you to your food?" he asked, his voice gravelly but his blue eyes steady. "I enjoy your company very much, but do not mean to intrude where I'm not wanted."

"Sit." Rather than point to the low, plush chairs meant for customers along the other wall, she slid a wooden stool under the counter so that he could share it with her. Her heart pounded. It was the first time she'd invited someone to share her space. She tried not to think about what that might mean. Instead, she turned her back to retrieve plates and cutlery from a shelf. "What did you bring?"

His grin was back, as sudden as lightning and just as devastating.

"I have no idea," he said cheerfully, and began to unpack the parcels. "At the mention of your name, everyone seems to know exactly what I should take."

Angelica tensed, expecting a sharp twinge of fear or embarrassment at the knowledge a raffish Scotsman had been out and about, linking his name with hers.

No such twinges occurred. He must have massaged them away.

Mr. MacLean retrieved a bottle of champagne from his satchel. "Shall we?"

She narrowed her eyes. "Champagne is for celebrations."

"You can use your hand again," he pointed out. "Huzzah!"

"I'm at work." She slid a single glass across the counter for him to use.

He shrugged. "Then I'll drink all of it. I'm on holiday. Veuve Clicquot seems just the thing."

Blast him. She slid a second glass across the counter. He filled them both.

He waited until she lifted hers before touching the rims of their wine glasses together. "To my favorite jeweler. *Slàinte!*"

"To hyperbolic strangers," she countered. "A toast to you."

He grinned, undaunted, and sipped his champagne.

The bubbles tickled her nose as she swallowed the tart sweetness. It was unfair of him to be so charming. The silver lining was that he would be gone within a fortnight, and she knew it. They could share meals. They could even be friends. But that was all it would be.

Her heart was firmly under lock and key.

"Well then, Miss Parker." He paused with his fork halfway to his mouth. "May I call you Angelica?"

"No, Mr. MacLean, you may not."

"I'm Jonathan," he reminded her. "Here's my question. How much champagne do you think it would take for us to 'accidentally' kiss?"

Her breath caught.

"There's not enough wine in England," she replied tartly, begging forgiveness to the heavens for her fib.

She was tempted at this very moment.

His smile indicated she needn't have bothered lying.

"Tell me about your day while you eat," she commanded, rushing to stave off this line of thought. "While you're talking, I'm going to eat as fast as I can so that I can return to the work I'm supposed to be completing."

Far from being offended, Mr. MacLean launched into a dramatic, no doubt highly embellished retelling of every encounter he'd had from the moment he woke up until he walked through her door.

Angelica could barely consume any food, for fear of snorting it out of her nose with laughter at his impressions of her fellow villagers and his own exaggerated reactions. He made the simple act of walking down the street seem like an odyssey.

She was surprised how much a part of her wished she had nothing else to do this week other than go pleasure-seeking all through Cressmouth, on Mr. MacLean's fashionable arm.

Meals were more diverting with him on the other side of the counter. She *liked* his nonsense.

"That's it for me." She pushed her plate aside and walked back to the piece she'd been working on. "You may continue talking. The buzz of noise *is* oddly comforting."

"Why, that's something *else* we have in common," he said with delight. "We both adore the sound of my voice! I have endless stories to tell. I wouldn't need to repeat any, whether you listen or not."

Angelica fought to keep amusement from curving her lips as she unfolded the black velvet from her work.

"Aye, I needed a purpose," he said in wonder, as though she'd handed him the answers to the universe, "and you've just given it to me. We can spend all your working hours together! Me, having a right blether, and you... well, *working*."

She pointedly neither replied nor glanced at him. Mostly to hide her smile.

"Oh!" he said, followed by the sound of rustling. "I could read to you from one of your books."

All right, that did it.

Angelica turned toward him. "What books?"

"I brought you these from the castle circulating library." He placed three leather volumes on the counter next to her work.

She picked up the first one. "*A Geologist's Guide to Igneous, Sedimentary, and Metamorphic Rock.*"

"Dull, isn't it?" He made a face. "I could read it to you at night so that you fall asleep faster."

The thought stole her breath and painted a picture far more appealing than she dared to let on.

"The guide is about jewels, you beast." She pointed at her chest. "Jeweler?"

His nose wrinkled. "Perhaps if it were more of a masked-villains-steal-the-Crown-Jewels-and-escape-in-a-floating-barrel sort of plot..."

She picked up the next book and a smile broke out over her face. Before her uncle had become a sought-after traveling preacher, he had read tales to her from this volume.

"Oh, dear," said Mr. MacLean. "How are you going to ignore me properly if the mere thought of that one makes you giddy?"

Splendid point.

She set it aside and picked up the third and

final book. It was a collection of songs and dance music, written and compiled by Ignatius Sancho.

"I have a dreadful singing voice," Mr. Mac-Lean warned her. "But you did say you liked noise. Is Mr. Sancho a famous British musician?"

She pressed the book to her bosom. "You don't know who Ignatius Sancho is?"

"Plays the pianoforte?" he guessed. "Flute? Tin whistle? Or is he more of a bagpipes-and-lute sort of fellow?"

This was why she could indulge no flights of fancy toward Mr. MacLean. It had nothing to do with her work commitments, or him being a passing tourist. They were too different.

"Ignatius Sancho was born into slavery in the middle of the sea on a crowded slave ship. He learnt to read and later became a butler, a composer, an actor, a shopkeeper… and an important leader and source of knowledge for abolitionists, due to his many writings about the atrocities of slavery. He was the first Black man known to vote in our parliamentary elections. I have a two-volume copy of his collected letters, if you'd like to read them."

"I think I would like to," Mr. MacLean said, surprising her. "Thank you."

"Everyone should read them. You've traveled extensively. In how many places have you seen fair and equitable treatment of Black people?"

"I've only traveled Scotland and England," he answered, his eyes serious. "And I can't say that those are the words I would use to describe what I've seen."

She inclined her head. At least he was honest.

"London is likely both the best and the worst," he mused. "Outside of aristocratic circles, there's a fairly large population of free Black people, as well as people from any number of countries and cultures. But beyond London, I've not seen many thriving communities, much less many examples of coexisting in a way I'd claim resembled 'fair and equitable.' Abolition is the only ethical stance, but of course just the beginning."

Angelica handed back the books. She respected Mr. MacLean for not only being able to see the truth, but to say it. One did not always like the things the truth exposed.

"My relatives cannot stand that I live so far away," she confessed. "There are other people of African descent here in Cressmouth, but of course not as many as London. Until they came to visit, my family didn't believe me when I insisted my fellow villagers generally treat us with the same respect they'd give any other neighbor. We're not just welcome here. Cressmouth belongs to all of us."

Mr. MacLean tilted his head in speculation. "What about the tourists?"

"Many of them are wonderful." They delighted in her creations and lined her pockets with gold. "Some of them treat all of us like quaint menagerie specimens, regardless of color." But their coins spent just the same as any other.

"As for the rest..." She lifted a shoulder. "The bad ones aren't any worse than the knaves you'd find anywhere else."

"That seems a low bar to clear," he murmured. His gaze held hers. "Are you happy here?"

Happy? What was happy? She hadn't been happy in London, and she was too busy to worry about such things here. She was happy once a year, when her family came up to spend Yuletide in the castle.

She'd be with them now if it weren't for all this work. An hour or two with her cousins and nieces and nephews in the evenings before falling into bed exhausted wasn't nearly enough time.

Soon, she promised herself. She'd be finished with her responsibilities by Christmas and could enjoy her family until Twelfth Night.

"Read aloud from whichever one you like." She picked up her tools, then paused. "What made you choose Ignatius Sancho if you didn't know who he was?"

"Oh, I didn't choose him. He was foisted upon me, along with the metamorphic rock and the parables. I was going to bring you *The Venetian Sorceress* or *The Castle of Wolfenbach*. I might be able to quote them by heart, if you like."

"Foisted upon you?" she repeated. "How does one find oneself the unwilling recipient of guides for geologists?"

"Due to an ill-tempered cat," he replied earnestly, "and a particular young lady who looks a bit like..." He pulled a notebook and a pencil from an inner waistcoat pocket and sketched a few lines on one of the pages. "…*this*."

He faced the notebook in her direction.

Angelica's friend Virginia gazed back at her as though she'd posed for the portrait.

Something Virginia would never do.

"I cannot believe you drew that so quickly!"

"I don't know her name," he explained, "which made this the most expedient way to convey her identity."

"Expedient?" she sputtered. "Why didn't you tell me you were an artist?"

He looked at her in surprise. "I'm not an artist. Artists carry arty things about. I have a pencil and a notebook, and sometimes I draw things." He seemed to think this over. "I *will* have to paint a few dozen illustrations when my business partner arrives." He shook his head. "An anomaly. My watercolors won't be part of the real catalogue. We'll employ a skilled professional once everything goes through."

She pursed her lips. "I haven't seen you paint, but if your efforts are anywhere near as 'amateur' as that portrait you just sketched, something smells of false modesty."

"No, no, no." His eyes widened earnestly. "I'm unquestionably talented at art. But I'm not an *artist*. I'm a wanderer. I *wander*. It may or may not be what I do best, but it's who I am."

Her fingers embossed mistletoe into the adornment. "Is that why you're here? You wandered into town, and then into my shop?"

"In a sense. I wandered into your shop that first day, and then kept coming back because I liked what I found. I wouldn't have chosen Cressmouth, but I needed an audience with Nottingvale, and I've already been to London. I won't visit the same town twice," he added, as though that explained anything.

Or perhaps it did. Maybe that last aside was meant to remind them both that he would soon be gone and would not be coming back.

"Don't you ever want to stay in one place?"

"I have a noble mission," he replied without hesitation. "My constant travels are what will initially spread the news—and the excitement—about Fit for a Duke."

"And then after that?"

"Growth will be self-sustaining, with or without my help." From the corner of her eye, she watched him sketch idly in his notebook.

"I meant, and then you'll find something else to do?"

"Finding things is my specialty." His pencil flew across the page. "That's how Fit for a Duke began—I found Calvin. Before that, it was clockmaking. And before that, ormolu-weaving. That's the best part of roving about. I find people who aren't as successful as they ought to be. I invest in them, which pays off for everyone. What price is ten percent for a year, when they're suddenly earning dozens or even a hundred times more than they were before?"

Angelica set a trio of paste diamonds in silence. She was impressed despite herself. Providing opportunities to those who would not otherwise have them was not something she could criticize. It was what she had always wanted for herself, and precisely how she'd ended up in Cressmouth... with terms that had cost her years with her family.

This time, she would succeed on her own.

"Wait," she said. "You didn't say your friend was going to owe you ten percent for a year. You called him your business partner."

"You're right," he admitted. "This one isn't temporary. Fit for a Duke is special. Nottingvale will own a small percent, and Calvin and I will split the rest."

"What makes this different? It looks more profitable?"

He waved a hand as though money were the least of his concerns. "It has the potential to be *ubiquitous*. If everything goes to plan, five years from now—maybe less—everyone in Britain will have heard of us." His eyes glittered. "If a catalogue for a company I've created is on everyone's table, no one can deny my success."

Oh, Angelica wasn't too sure about that. Other people had all sorts of ways to decide you weren't living up to your potential. Even those who meant well. There were plenty of friends and family members who thought her unnatural because she'd chosen to run a jeweler's shop instead of starting a family.

But she understood what drove him. The

wish for status, for unarguable proof of her worth. All the people who thought nothing of asking her when she was going to be a wife wouldn't think so little of her talent if her jewelry was the talk of England.

As it was, her shop was barely the talk of her village. Wasn't that why she'd agreed to take on more projects than she had time for? Once her jeweled holly sprigs were the stars of the Christmas festivities, and her name was featured in the *Cressmouth Gazette*, she too would have something to hold up and point to whenever someone dared question her success.

"You'd never go back to London?" she asked.

"I've been there before."

"Have you been *everywhere* in London?" she challenged. "What about Fournier Street in Spitalfields?"

Rather than reply, he flipped to a new page in his notebook and sketched long, sweeping lines, followed by a flurry of shorter, lighter strokes. He held up the page when he finished.

Her pulse scattered.

It was her old neighborhood. Exactly as it had looked the year before she'd moved to Cressmouth. The same homes, the same shops. Her family's awning was right there at the edge of the paper. Her breath caught as a white-hot burst of homesickness shot through her.

"What is it?" he asked, concerned.

"I spent the first twenty years of my life right there." She pointed with her cross-pein hammer.

"I have two communities. Cressmouth is one, and that's the other."

She regretted it as soon as she said it. It sounded like bragging. She had two homes, and he had none.

Even if he liked it that way, she could not help but feel sorry for him.

He tucked the notebook in his pocket.

"What are you going to do for Christmas?" she asked.

"Nothing," he said flatly. "Wander to the next town."

His tone closed the topic. Not that she had more to say. What was she to do, invite him to join *her* family holiday? She could just imagine the looks on their faces. Besides, Mr. MacLean was standing in the most Christmassy village in all of England. If he hadn't found anything yet that tempted him, Angelica's invitation wasn't going to.

"What about you?" he asked. "Would you go back to London?"

"In a heartbeat. But I don't know if I'd stay. Ironically, I have more opportunities here." She adjusted her swage. "When I met Mr. Marlowe, his Christmas castle was already a brilliant success, but it wasn't enough. He wanted an entire Yuletide village. To do that, Cressmouth needed to offer everything any tourist might desire."

"Not just practical needs, like a blacksmith, a bakery, a dairy," Mr. MacLean said slowly. "He wasn't competing with other villages. He was competing with London. He needed to offer the best of the best, so that people needn't *decide* between seasonal destinations. There'd be no choice to make, if Cressmouth was the obvious answer."

"Which was why it was flattering for Mr. Marlowe to choose *me*," Angelica said. The expressions on her family's faces had been unforgettable. "Of course, no dreams come true for free."

He raised his brows. "Mr. Marlowe charged you money to move from London to this tiny village?"

"He didn't, actually. He gave me a private suite in the castle, and free use of this shop. If I left Cressmouth before seven years were through—left for any reason, for even a single night—the arrangement was off, and I would owe rent on both places for every day that I'd been here. But if I stayed the seven years, both the shop and the castle living quarters would be mine outright."

"That son-of-a..." Mr. MacLean coughed into his fist. "You couldn't have so much as a holiday. Leaving would beggar you."

She nodded. "But the cost wasn't just monetary. I missed the birth of my niece, the death of a childhood friend. My relatives don't understand. Oh, they comprehend the mechanics of the agreement, and how well it ties my hands. What they don't understand is why I signed it."

"Would you have had a shop of your own if you'd stayed in London?"

"Not even a workbench," she said quietly.

"Then *I* understand why you signed. You wanted to be yourself. To be self-sufficient. To do something you were passionate about, and proud of." His eyes were bright. "In your shoes, I would have signed it, too."

She shook her head. "Family is supposed to come *first*."

He frowned. "Then why wouldn't *you* have come first, to them? Aren't you family, too?"

She stared back at him, speechless. It was not an argument that had ever been made on her behalf before.

"I'm part of the family," she stammered. "Because I can't spend Christmastide with them, they come up and stay in the castle. You'd be surprised how many aunts and cousins can fit in one suite. The exorbitant prices that castle charges tourists for a single night's stay... Instead, they have free lodgings, free food, and free entertainment because of me. It's a holiday they could never have dreamed of, if I hadn't signed that agreement. They wouldn't have this opportunity without me."

"That's not what you want, is it?" His gaze held hers. "You don't want to be the person they visit because of a free room at the inn. You want to be the cousin they're proud to be related to because she's a talented jeweler worthy of admiration and respect."

"It'll be seven years this Christmas," she said with a sigh. "I thought I'd be a success by now."

"Aren't you?" His voice was softer. Closer. He was no longer tucked safely at the other end of the long counter, but leaning on his elbow at a distance close enough to touch. "You look like a successful woman to me."

She didn't answer. Her throat was too dry.

"Your friend didn't ask you to design ten important adornments at the last minute because you're the only jeweler in Cressmouth," he continued. "She asked because she knew you would succeed. That whatever you created would be worth writing about in the newspaper. She came to you because you're splendid at what you do."

Her fingers shook. She set down the hammer and swage.

He reached for her hand.

She placed hers in his without question.

He brought her fingers to his lips and pressed a soft, slow kiss to her knuckles without taking his eyes from hers. Then he cradled her trembling palm in his and began to massage the muscles. It should have been presumptuous. Instead, it was perfect.

Had she claimed there wasn't enough wine in England for them to kiss? She was beginning to think there was no force in England powerful enough to stop it from happening.

Not that Mr. MacLean would be stealing anything. If Angelica found herself in his arms...

It would be because she'd launched herself there willingly.

CHAPTER 7

*B*y the fifth day of being snowed in, in a tiny village, with no hope of escape, Jonathan would have expected to be going none-too-quietly mad.

Instead, he was perched on a wooden stool at the long oak counter in Miss Parker's jeweler's shop. He read aloud from a leather-bound collection of Ignatius Sancho's letters whenever Miss Parker was between customers and trying to concentrate on the adornments she was making for the upcoming Yuletide ball at Marlowe Castle.

According to her, Jonathan's rugged, manly Scottish burr was the perfect tone and volume to disregard completely whilst molding gold or setting jewels. Of course, this was said with a smile. Far from ignoring his endless chatter, she seemed to truly enjoy it. Not with casual amusement, as a hackney driver or haberdasher might. Miss Parker listened carefully. She *wanted* to hear

Jonathan's stories. She *liked* his chatter. It was dizzying.

The frequent conversations that punctuated today's readings were just as interesting and elucidating as the text itself. Jonathan found himself engaging with the material—with Miss Parker—on a level far more profound than his usual superficial interactions. He wasn't talking *at* her. These discussions were something they did together.

Jonathan tried to pretend that entertainment was the only reason he was doing this: perhaps to learn something whilst distracting himself from his wintry plight.

But the truth was, it didn't feel like a plight. He looked forward to each new morning, because it was another opportunity to see Miss Parker. If she asked it of him, he would have climbed atop his stool and quoted geology texts all day. He liked watching her work.

He liked watching her, full stop.

Her tight black curls, escaping what was meant to be a severe, no-nonsense bun. Her wide brown eyes, framed by curling black lashes. Her dimpled cheeks and kissable lips. The column of her throat, her pulse fluttering at the base. The soft brown skin that invited his touch. The swell of her bosom, displayed to advantage in a pale pink bodice. Just beneath it, the satin ribbon that encircled her ribs. The long, billowing pink skirts that merely hinted at the ample curves beneath.

He could scarcely look at her without his heart thumping wildly.

Jonathan must have stopped reading aloud. Miss Parker wasn't looking at the beautiful piece she was crafting in her hands, but rather across the counter at him.

He should have moved the stool much farther than an arm's length away. If he put down the book and moved his hand a little to the right, and if she moved hers a little to his left, their fingers would touch.

It shouldn't feel salacious. He touched her fingers twice a day now, to massage the tension from her hands. He longed to continue his exploratory path up her palms, past her wrists, to the tender skin on the inside of her forearms. He wanted to feel her cheek in his hand, her bodice pressed against him, her curves beneath his palms.

This was why he did not let go of the book, although he'd completely forgotten whatever line he'd last read aloud. He was here to help her work, not to daydream about kissing her.

And yet he leaned closer. Just a little bit. He kept a tight enough grip on the book to turn his fingers white—it shielded them both—but he did tilt ever so slightly further across the scarred oak, like a sapling rising to meet the sun.

Now she seemed closer than she should be. Closer than he'd expected. When he'd leaned toward her, she must have done the same. Their lips were still at an unkissable distance, but that was nothing a moment of madness couldn't cure.

If he set down the book, perhaps she'd set down her tools. And if she set down the tools, perhaps he'd take her hands in his. And if he took her hands in his, he'd bring them to his lips, one finger at a time. And then once he'd kissed them all, he'd press those soft hands to his galloping heart and cover her mouth with his.

It was a terrible idea.

A wonderful idea.

She set down her tool.

His heart banged against his ribcage. He should not do any of the things he was currently desperate to do. Not only could a customer walk in at any moment... Jonathan was *leaving*, and they both knew it. A kiss of any kind, no matter how chaste, was a promise he could not fulfill.

He cleared his throat.

She became inordinately interested in a tiny hammer.

His chest ached. He wondered what would have happened if he hadn't ruined the moment. Whether they would have regretted the transgression.

Whether it would have been worth it anyway.

He shook his head. Whatever this was between them would have to remain platonic. Friendship, nothing more. Even if the snow forced him to stay in Cressmouth for months, he knew better than to allow the ice about his heart to melt.

Jonathan still remembered the pain when those who were *supposed* to love him decided they were better off without him. There was never time for Jonathan. Those he loved, *left*. He wouldn't set himself up to be hurt like that again. He wouldn't let himself be hurt at all.

Polite acquaintances. That was the best thing. Then leaving wouldn't hurt.

"Mayhap we need jewelry," he blurted out.

She gestured about her shop without looking up. "We're surrounded by jewelry."

"Not you and I," he said. "I mean Fit for a Duke. Calvin is the most talented tailor I've ever had the good fortune to meet, but what of the men not in the market for an entire ensemble? Mightn't they still desire a small, fashionable touch?"

He was babbling. Why was he babbling? Because he was making this up as he went along. Because he wasn't thinking about "some men." He wasn't thinking about customers at all. He was thinking of himself, and how much he wished he could keep a piece of her with him when he left.

"Signet rings," he said. No—too fancy, and inherently personal. "Cravat pins. Small, but elegant. Affordable."

What was he talking about? No one in their right mind would pore over a catalogue for the privilege of purchasing a cravat pin.

It was Jonathan who longed for a secret memento. Something to keep hidden from view, close to his heart. Something he could easily explain away, if confronted by his own sentimentality.

"Not a cravat pin," she said slowly, as though his self-conscious rush of prattle held actual worth. "A ring is too ostentatious, and a pin isn't special enough. But there must be something that would do. It's a good idea. I'll think about what you might do."

"Don't worry about my project," he said quickly. "You have enough to do without me adding to it."

She sent him a droll look. "Would it surprise you to learn I can think and hammer a *repoussé* relief at the same time?"

His neck heated. "Sometimes I do a poor job of thinking, even when it's the only thing I'm trying to do."

The edges of her lips quirked. "I doubt that very much. You may be a peculiar sort, I'll grant you that, but if even half your stories are true, you're clever and compassionate."

"And selfish," he reminded her. "I do it for money."

"Do you?" Her brown eyes looked as though she could see through to his soul.

He opened his mouth.

Nothing came out.

Silence? From the man who claimed to be an open book? No one had ever asked him anything *serious* before. Perhaps his thoughts on figs or rain or boot-polish. No one probed to get past the glib answer, the light repartee. He wasn't sure he liked it. He didn't know how to react.

Miss Parker returned her gaze to her chisel.

"You were right," she said. "When you guessed I wanted to prove myself all by myself. My brother is a jeweler, too. He's not allowed in my shop until it *is* my shop, and I can say, 'Everything you see here is mine. *I* made it. *I* earned it. I'm successful.'" She glanced up, but her smile didn't meet her eyes. "All that work has led to some very lonely moments." She arched a brow. "I can admit it. Can you?"

He'd challenged himself to risk making a true connection.

"Life can be lonely," he admitted. "Even when surrounded by new people to meet." Perhaps especially then. "Calvin is the first partner I've ever had. It's terrifying, and we've not even signed an agreement with the duke yet. It won't change my life in any measurable way. It shouldn't be frightening. I'll still travel as much as I want, go wherever I wish. And yet, tying myself to him makes my success seem *less* mine. As though I haven't earned it. As though it doesn't count."

"And the loneliness?" she prodded.

Ah. He'd skipped past that, hadn't he.

"It's the way it must be," he said simply. "I'm never anywhere long enough to see the actual impact of the thing I'm selling, to hear what anyone actually thinks, to make friends or even meaningful connections. And yet, if I *don't* keep moving, the project I'm trying to advertise will reach fewer people, will have less momentum, a lower chance of success. Calvin is the brains behind Fit for a Duke's fashions. I'm the feet that brings them to the people."

He felt like he was balancing on a precipice.

Or rather, not balancing. Windmilling his arms wildly, in a desperate attempt to stay upright long after gravity had begun to win the fight.

She nodded. "That's how I felt when I told my family about the agreement I'd made. The terms felt like more than anyone had a right to ask of me, and at the same time, my only chance to use my potential. And once I set out on that path, I had to continue."

He tilted his head. "You're exceptional. Mr. Marlowe was clever enough to recognize a hidden gem when he saw it. Cressmouth is his crown, and you its diamond. Even if all he could have were seven years, I'd wager he's been gloating over his good fortune every minute of it."

"But *am* I self-made if someone else made it all possible?" Her eyes were haunted. "Or should I have stayed home with my family? Been the sort of daughter they had hoped for?"

"You're the sort of woman anyone would hope for," he said and meant it. "The question you're asking happens to be my particular expertise. Someone investing in you doesn't mean you have less worth, but *more*. It means faith. You should believe in yourself, too."

Her hands were in his. Had she placed them there? Or had he reached for her, during his impassioned speech?

It didn't matter. He pressed each soft knuckle to his lips just as he'd dreamt of doing, then placed her palms one atop the other over his heart. He had never kissed anyone with an oak counter standing between them, but this seemed a perfect moment to start.

His blood thrummed. He caressed her cheek, lightly, softly. Drawing her in, but only if she wanted to come.

She leaned forward, tilting her face into his hand, toward him.

He brushed his mouth over hers, once, twice, then kissed her fully. Completely. He, too, could spot a diamond. But he didn't want to take anything from her. He wanted to give. All the kisses she could desire, all the massages, all the shared moments, from the silly to the serious and everything in between. He couldn't stop kissing her. Not when she returned his kisses so sweetly.

But he had no right to such liberties. They had no agreement, no understanding, no future once the snow ceased to fall. A single kiss was one too many. A risk neither of them should have been foolish enough to take.

He pulled his mouth from hers whilst he still had the wherewithal to do so. He turned away before she noticed his discomfort. This was a lovely time to go and stand outside in the freezing weather. A perfect time. It was exactly what he was going to do.

"Biscuits," he mumbled, because there was no possibility he was going to discuss the kisses they'd shared. "I'll just pop across the street for some... biscuits."

He was out through the door and out into the lightly falling snow before he realized he'd left behind his hat and scarf and coat. But if he couldn't be trusted to keep his hands off Miss Parker, he deserved to freeze his fingers and everything else.

Thanks to his efforts along with the volunteer crew, now the pavements were tidy and the road clear from shovels and sleighs. One needn't trudge through knee-high snow to cross the street... until morning, when the shoveling would begin anew.

"There he is!" Mr. Bauer chortled when Jonathan walked through the door. "We wondered what mischief you had got up to."

"Look!" Stephen leaned against the windowsill and stuck out his leg, brandishing his foot this way and that. "I'm ready to go sledding again!"

"So you are," Jonathan said. "Aim away from the trees."

Mr. Bauer handed him two parcels. "There you are, then. The first one has extras of the biscuits you like best. The other has Miss Parker's favorite pie."

The parcel was in Jonathan's hands before he

realized he hadn't even ordered yet. The baker remembered him, noted his absence. Wondered what he'd got up to.

It was a heady sensation. He'd never been a regular customer anywhere before. It was rather nice. Rather more than nice. A sinking sensation filled his stomach.

Jonathan was going to miss Cressmouth.

His muscles tightened. He left a pile of coins on the counter for the baker, and tossed a sovereign to Stephen on his way through the door. It must be just as cold out as it was a few minutes ago, but it didn't feel like it. Not after the warmth of the bakery, in more ways than one.

He was thinking about Angelica. And his secret dream that, one day, he would find someone who would ask him to stay.

The sound of laughter caused him to jerk his gaze toward the castle. A man about Jonathan's age with black hair and brown skin was pulling two little girls down the hill on wooden sleds. The fresh snow was too high to slide properly, but their obvious merriment indicated it was no less enjoyable.

Jonathan wondered if the family were part of the local Black community Miss Parker had mentioned, or if they were tourists, like him. He called out a greeting as they sledded by.

"Ho, there! The baker's son has an itch to race sleds, if you're up for it."

"Can't," one of the girls called back. "We're on our way to see the horses!"

The man stopped in his tracks, making a big show of stretching out his presumably tired arms from dragging the girls up and down the hill.

Jonathan handed him one of the parcels. "If your arms aren't *too* tired, you can share biscuits and shortbread amongst yourselves."

The man peeked under the brown paper and grinned back at him.

"Share?" he said in a voice clearly meant to carry to his daughters. "*I'm* the one who's been treated like a horse. I think all these delicious, fresh biscuits should be for me."

Both girls squealed and leapt up from their sleds, holding out wool mittens in hopes of a sugared treat.

Their father placed a single biscuit in each pair of outstretched mittens and handed the rest back to Jonathan.

"It's yours. I've got mine." Jonathan held up the parcel with the pie. "I suspect those two know what to do with a dozen biscuits."

"*Share* them," their father intoned with faux sternness. "With your cousins."

"Nooo," they cried, jumping up and down. "Just one more! Just two more!"

"Thank you," said their father to Jonathan. "Happy Christmas to you."

That was enough to make Jonathan's smile fall. Despite the snow, he'd forgotten for a moment where they were, and what time of the year it was.

"A happy Christmas to you, too." He turned toward Miss Parker's shop.

"Off to buy some jewelry, are you?" said the man.

"No," Jonathan said without thinking. "Off to share a pie with... a friend."

The girls stopped fighting over the biscuits. They and their father stared at Jonathan as though he'd turned into a hobgoblin.

"You're going to share a pie with my sister?" the man asked, his tone dangerous.

Oh, dear. Jonathan froze in place. Now that he said so, the family resemblance was clear. So was Mr. Parker's obvious anger. Was it too late for Jonathan to pretend he was the baker's delivery man?

"Aunt doesn't allow friends and family in her shop," said the first girl.

"Only customers," agreed the second.

The man swept his cold gaze over him. "If she lets *you* loiter, she should let *me* in. At least I'm an expert."

Jonathan matched his frosty tone. "*She* should do whatever she likes. It's her shop. Her rules."

The man snorted, as if Jonathan had made a jest. "You sound just like her. She acts as though this little shop—"

"Whatever she's said about the shop, she's underselling it," Jonathan cut in. "Your sister is extraordinarily talented, and more than deserving of both respect and proper accolades. She may be one of the most skilled jewelers in England."

"Papa is the most skilled," said the first little girl.

"Papa told us so," agreed the second.

Brilliant. No wonder Miss Parker didn't allow her brother inside.

Angelica faced away from the counter and touched her fingers to her mouth. Mr. MacLean had kissed each of her ten fingers, one by one, before attending to her mouth just as thoroughly.

She shouldn't have let him do it.

She shouldn't have let him *stop*.

He'd come to his senses faster than she had, and run off in a manner that would be comical... if she didn't feel his absence all the way to her bones. The air was colder without him.

What would it be like when he left for good?

Her fingers curled into a fist and she sank her teeth into a knuckle. She did not wish to think about him leaving. She didn't wish to think about him at all. She was *busy*. There was no time for romantical entanglements.

Yes, they got along uncomfortably well, and yes, he had started to feel like part of her town, but the latter, at least, was an illusion. He was part of *every* town for a few days, and then he moved on. He would move on from here as well. He had been forthright about his intentions. Though she appreciated his frankness, the warning was unnecessary.

Angelica was long used to locking away inconsequential desires in order to concentrate on what mattered most: her work. The Christmastide adornments she'd been commissioned to create, the sundry jewelry pieces that were next on the list.

She turned back to face her counter just as the bell tinkled over the door.

It wasn't a customer. It was Mr. MacLean. He had rushed out into the cold without a hat or coat like a damn fool, yet his ruffled hair and wind-reddened face didn't make him any less attractive.

She pretended it was the meal in his hands and not the man himself that awakened a hunger in her belly.

To hide her own strangely flushed cheeks, she busied herself arranging plates and silverware on their usual dining corner of the counter.

"No wine for me," she said firmly. "I'm finishing the last of the adornments today. The ball is tomorrow."

He set the pie on the counter next to the plates. Rather than take his seat on the wooden stool, he glanced over her shoulder at the clock behind her and winced.

She arched a brow. "Have you got somewhere to be?"

"I hoped not," he said. "But I think your brother is waiting for me to reappear, to settle our argument."

The fork in Angelica's hand clattered to the oak counter. "My who? Your *what?*"

Mr. MacLean shrugged into his coat. "I told him not to worry; I'm not trying to steal his sister. Let me see what he wants."

No way was she leaving the two of them alone.

Angelica hurried to swing open the counter's hinged access panel, but by the time she was on the other side, Mr. MacLean was already out through the door.

She hesitated with her hand on the cold brass handle.

Luther was there, square jaw tilted stubbornly, the edges of two frayed ropes poking up from his gloved fists.

The ropes led to two wooden sleds, upon which her nieces Florence and Esther were happily consuming an exorbitant quantity of biscuits.

Had she thought to avoid potential trouble by not introducing Mr. MacLean to her relatives? Ha. She'd forgotten just how small this village was. Cressmouth had a single street leading in or out. All of the businesses were on it. And Mr. MacLean introduced himself to everyone.

Angelica had wondered what he and her

family would make of each other? Well, she was about to find out.

She pulled on her coat and rushed outside into wisps of snow.

"You allow this… *Scot* to loiter in your shop?" Luther demanded.

Angelica understood her brother's suspicion and confusion. She wouldn't have believed it herself just a couple weeks earlier.

For now, she settled on a simple, "Yes."

"I'm your brother," Luther sputtered. "We lived together, learnt the trade together, worked side-by-side our whole lives… until you decided to abandon the family and move to the north of England to please some eccentric rich man rather than your own mama. But I never believed you'd prefer some… aristocratic *nob* over your own blood."

"Want a biscuit, Aunt Angelica?" Florence asked.

"Not now, darling," she murmured.

Angelica had known her relatives did not understand her. They'd come to accept her decision, even to enjoy its peripheral fruits, but there was no hyperbole in her brother's words when he said the family believed she had abandoned them.

Luther, specifically, felt hurt and slighted. They had not just grown up together. After their father died, Luther became the man of the house. Their aunts were respected elders, but Luther was the one who owned their home, their shop.

He was the important sibling.

Angelica was the little sister. The one her father had taught his craft to, not because he had intended to, but because she never left her elder brother's shadow.

She'd learned despite them, not because of them.

The first falling-out between her and her brother was the day their father had said, "No, Luther! Look how Angelica's accomplished it."

The *worst* falling-out she'd had with her brother was the day their father pronounced Angelica the better jeweler... and said it didn't matter. She was destined to be a wife, not an artisan. She inherited the talent, but Luther inherited the shop.

None of which was likely to ever be properly resolved. She and Luther had loved each other and been jealous of each other for far too long to change now.

Mr. MacLean's omnipresent grin was absent from his usually cheerful face. Perhaps his perpetually sunny disposition wasn't his true self, but rather his shield. Just like refusing to let people in was hers.

"I liked your biscuits," said Florence.

Esther nodded, her mouth full. "Thank you for sharing them."

"My pleasure," Mr. MacLean murmured without meeting Angelica's eyes.

Of course the biscuits were his. That was exactly how he was. He would have tried to make a good impression on her brother and her nieces without even knowing they were her family.

If anyone was making a bad impression, it was Angelica. That the two men had squared off like cockerels in a cockfight was their problem, but her refusal to blend the different parts of her life wasn't making the situation any better.

She blinked. Did she now consider him part of her life? No. He was temporary. But something had to be done.

"It's good you ran into each other," she said. "I meant to introduce you."

Miraculously, no lightning bolt struck her where she stood.

"This is Mr. MacLean, my... friend. He's only passing through."

"Jonathan MacLean, at your service." He made an extravagant leg, fit for a king.

Florence and Esther exchanged impressed glances.

"And this is my brother Mr. Luther Parker, and his daughters Florence and Esther."

Luther folded his arms over his chest. "Your friend, is he? I'm sure the rest of the family would just love to meet him. Why don't you take him to church on Sunday? Uncle is giving a service at the castle."

"Sunday?" she squeaked.

"Uncle's Christmas service," Florence piped up helpfully.

Esther pumped her hands in the air. "Everyone will be there!"

The gauntlet had been thrown.

"All right." Angelica met her brother's eyes. "If Mr. MacLean wishes to come to church, he's welcome to join us."

Luther looked as though a gentle snowflake could have knocked him down.

Angelica didn't blame him.

If she sat next to Mr. MacLean at Sunday service, she'd be laying claim to him in front of the entire village—and more importantly, in front of her entire family. If Luther had been surprised and confused, the looks on her aunts' and cousins' faces…

Fortunately, any apparent "claim" would be as transient as Mr. MacLean himself.

He was still leaving. Her relatives needn't know they had become *kissing* friends.

Though they might suspect as much.

"Horses!" Esther squealed, tugging on the rope in her father's gloved hand. "You promised!"

"Horses! Horses!" Florence chanted.

Luther bounced a final, skeptical look between Angelica and Mr. MacLean, then adjusted his grip on the ropes. "Are you still coming to visit us tonight, once you finish… working?"

"Yes," Florence said. "She's plaiting my hair."

"Plaiting mine first," Esther corrected.

"Of course I am," Angelica agreed. "I've an appointment to plait hair."

Her brother touched his hat. "We'll discuss things then."

He pulled the sleds down the hill.

Angelica's heart pounded. She felt more in over her head than ever.

Mr. MacLean's expression was unreadable. "Shall I leave you to your work?"

That was like him, too. Asking, rather than assuming.

Even before Luther had stuck his nose into her business, if she'd told Mr. MacLean never to speak to her again, Angelica had no doubt he would have respected her wishes. She let him keep coming back because she *wanted* him to be there.

"Don't be silly," she said. "We've a pie waiting for us."

"I would never be disrespectful to a pie," he replied solemnly.

Or her, she realized. He had neither agreed to nor declined the Sunday invitation. He would want to choose the path that would please her most, which would have been impossible to determine with all the silent accusations and recriminations flying between Angelica and her brother.

She owed Mr. MacLean an explanation.

But first, pie.

When the last crumbs were gone, she took the soiled dishes straight to the sink to collect her thoughts for a moment. Her house was as tidy as she could keep it, but her familial relations...

She pulled a stool over to Mr. MacLean's side of the counter.

"When the sale and purchase of humans became illegal in Britain, all existing slaves weren't magically set free. My grandfather was lucky. The man who'd owned him was last of his line, and freed my grandfather in his will. He didn't just gain his freedom, but the contents of the shop he'd been working in all his life as well. Of course, it wasn't easy. He moved everything to Spitalfields, and built up a new business, with new clientele. Our people."

Mr. MacLean listened quietly.

"Our community supports each other however we can. I was expected to help with womanly duties, and marry a nice, church-going man from the neighborhood. Luther was expected to help my father and to eventually take over the shop."

"Whether he had aptitude or not?" Mr. MacLean asked. He shook his head. "Or rather, whether your brother wished to or not."

Angelica stared at him. She had been so bitter for so long that Luther had had the family shop handed to him, that it hadn't occurred to her to wonder if he'd ever wanted it. Her father's will had been unquestionably unfair to Angelica, and perhaps just as unfair to her brother.

Inheriting responsibility for the shop was an emotional life sentence to a craft that had never brought him joy.

"He's good at it," she said, though that didn't make it better.

"The best, according to his daughters." Mr.

MacLean widened his eyes innocently. "He told them so himself."

Her mouth twitched. "He can keep dreaming."

But the fire had gone out from her. She and Luther had wasted so many years being jealous of each other when the truth was, they had far more similarities than differences.

Perhaps Luther wasn't angry she'd "abandoned" him. Perhaps he was bitter she'd gone after what she wanted, when he'd never had the opportunity to do the same.

Without Angelica or their father, Luther would have had to fend for himself. Trial by fire. He brought her a trinket every Christmas, and every time the workmanship had markedly improved.

He *was* talented. He'd been forced to become so.

"Don't worry," Mr. MacLean said. "I informed them you were one of the best in England."

She arched her brows. "Did Luther's mind explode?"

He nodded. "Top hat popped right off."

"I hope the girls weren't upset."

He shook his head. "Too busy eating biscuits."

She slid her hands over his. "I'm sorry you had to meet my brother like that."

He rubbed his thumbs over her palms. "We got on well enough until he realized I get on with you. He was probably afraid I was taking liberties."

Her gaze dropped to his mouth. "I like how you take liberties."

"Is that so? Then perhaps I needn't take them," he said. "If you want me to have any more liberties, you'll have to give them to me yourself."

"Watch me." She pressed her lips to his.

This kiss was different than the one before. Mr. MacLean was hesitant, unsure of his welcome. Angelica was determined to clear up any misunderstanding.

Just because he wouldn't stay was no reason not to enjoy a kiss or two whilst he was here. If anything, it made things easier. She had avoided men's company because she wasn't ready to be someone's wife.

But Mr. MacLean wasn't looking for marriage. He was not disappointed in her for indulging ambition. He understood. He would do the same. More importantly, he was the sort of person that would support her decision no matter what it was, just because it was her decision to make.

What could be more attractive than that?

She broke the kiss, but only moved far enough to look into his eyes.

"Miss Parker—"

"Angelica," she corrected.

He grinned. "Jonathan."

The next kiss was even sweeter.

She loved the way he cupped her face with the same gentle tenderness as when he first touched her hand. As though she were precious. She didn't *think* he expected more from her than kisses, but...

She broke the kiss again. "I'm not looking for a husband."

"I understand."

Did he? "I won't make love unless I'm married."

She had told him so before, but the terms bore repeating.

He nodded. "The chain of events is clear."

"And you still want to kiss me?"

"I'll never stop wanting to."

"It's only until the snow melts," she said. First-naming each other changed nothing. "When your business partner arrives..."

"I'll be too busy to think of anything but Fit for a Duke," he finished firmly. "And then I'll be gone. You're not the only one with big plans."

No. But Angelica was the one who suddenly wished their big plans didn't conflict. That he *could* stay. That she would have time for him if he did. That they could find an excuse for this to last longer than a fortnight.

That goodbye didn't have to be final.

He kissed her cheek rather than her lips. "Off to work, then. No more throwing your heaving bosom into my embrace until dinnertime."

"My heaving bosom is now a respectable distance from your waistcoat," she pointed out primly.

His eyes twinkled. "Aye, so you admit your bosom was heaving."

She smacked his shoulder before slipping around to the other side of the counter. Her lips couldn't stop smiling. He was incorrigible.

"Are you going to read or sketch today whilst I work?"

"I thought I'd share a wee bit o' Scotland." He held up a book and made a show of clearing his throat. "Robert Burns, *Address to a Haggis.*"

She covered her face with her hands. "You're lucky I don't actually listen to you."

But the truth was, she'd listen to him read anything. She loved the low, smooth timbre of his voice, the soft burr on his tongue.

"I almost forgot," she said as she set a string of paste rubies into the holly. "I thought of jewelry you could offer with Fit for a Duke."

The ode to haggis ceased abruptly. "Something better than a cravat pin?"

"A lover's locket." They were often beautiful gold capsules with a secret frame inside, bearing a tiny portrait of a loved one's eye. The locket could be worn as a brooch, or hung from a necklace next to one's heart.

She glanced up in time to see his jaw fall open with enthusiasm.

"That's brilliant," he breathed, abandoning Robert Burns to come and sit across from her. "Lover's lockets are all the rage, and can be fashioned in so many styles. Wheat, plumage, Greek..."

"Mosaic, cameo, intaglio..." At his blank look, she explained, "Designed with recessed engravings." She held up the adornment she was working on. "Like the texture of these leaves."

Jonathan pulled his notebook from his inner pocket and began madly scribbling notes. "They won't come with their lover's portrait inside, of course."

"Or the wisp of their lover's hair," she added with a grin. "But it could be designed in such a way that all your client need do is slip the lock of hair and partial portrait in place, and voilà. He can keep his lover hidden next to his heart."

"That's what we'll call it! 'The Duke's Secret.' Everyone will be clamoring for a locket of their own." His eyes shone with excitement. He could barely sit still. "When can you start?"

"When... what?" she stammered.

"Just a prototype," he said quickly. "Not thousands of them for all of England. I just need one to show Calvin and Nottingvale. If you're the one who designs it, they'll see the genius at once. No one else will do."

His confidence in her was simultaneously wonderful and terrifying. He clearly believed in her, thought no one else would do it justice. She wasn't interchangeable with any other jeweler. *Genius,* he'd called it.

It was the most flattering thing anyone had ever said about her talent.

But she had no time to add anything new to her already overworked days. She'd be lucky to plait her nieces' hair and manage a few hours' sleep before dawn came and she was in front of her worktable anew.

"I have to finish the last adornment tonight," she reminded him.

"After the indoor tree ceremony," he said. "I doubt the roads will be clear by then, even if it stops snowing tonight, which means we've plenty of time before Calvin and Nottingvale arrive."

"There's no time." She pointed at the unfinished piece on black velvet. "I've these pieces to finish as well, and…"

And if she believed in Jonathan even a fraction of as much as he believed in her, his catalogue was about to be far more widely read than Noelle's article in the *Cressmouth Gazette*.

She *did* believe in him, Angelica realized. He had his own brand of genius. And his excitement was infectious.

"I won't do it for free," she said. "If you want my work, you'll have to pay for it."

"Obviously." He didn't even glance up from his notebook. "Name your price."

She had the odd sensation that there was no number she could name that he wouldn't agree to out of hand. But that wasn't what she wanted. She was more ambitious than a lump sum payment and a handshake goodbye.

Instead of fighting their attraction, what if they worked together? Not temporarily, but for good?

"Ten percent," she said.

His head shot up from the notebook. "What?"

"Ten percent of the profit for every lover's locket sold from my designs."

She held her breath. What if he said no?

What if he said *yes?*

If her family had not understood any of her past decisions, they definitely would not understand if she suddenly canceled Christmas while they were right down the road, so that she could shutter herself in her workroom, designing lockets for a company that did not yet exist. She would lose the minimal time she had with them now.

But with ten percent of all future profits made from her designs, she would have *more* time to spend with her relatives, not less. She'd be able to visit them in London. Take them all on holiday wherever they wished. She could have the distinguished presence she'd been working toward as well as time to enjoy it.

If Jonathan said yes.

He narrowed his eyes. "Twelve."

She blinked. "What?"

"All right, fifteen," he said. "But only on the lockets you design, and of course only if my partners agree to it."

She couldn't believe her ears. "That means yes?"

"They'll be surprised," he said slowly, "but I don't see how they can deny the logic. Calvin shall receive a large percentage of the entire company's earnings based on his fashion designs, so why shouldn't you earn a portion of the profit we make off of *yours?* If they like your prototype, of course."

"They'll *adore* my prototype. They'll walk about with ten gold lockets strapped to their chests because they won't be able to decide which design they like best," she informed him.

"In that case," he said, "I suppose we're a team."

A *team.* Her heart skipped.

She hadn't worked with someone else since she moved to Cressmouth seven years ago. By Jonathan's own admission, this company was the first true partnership of his life.

Their futures were now tied together.

CHAPTER 9

The Marlowe Castle annual Yuletide ball started in less than an hour. Angelica hadn't moved for fifteen minutes.

She stood in front of her wardrobe, willing it to contain something other than six identical day dresses, two identical church dresses, and one tired evening gown.

Because she had spent most of the last seven years at her worktable, there had not been many appearances in ballrooms. Only during Yuletide, in fact, when her relatives came up from London.

They teased Angelica relentlessly for her uninspired wardrobe. Even though Luther knew his sister preferred to use her brain only for important decisions, he still loved to intimate that perhaps Angelica really did only own two dresses, and always offered to buy her one more just to "liven" her up.

Tonight was the first time she wished she'd let him.

She wouldn't have touched it until now, making it something new she could wear, just for Jonathan. Who would be here in... She glanced at the clock upon the mantel. Twenty minutes.

Well, she'd be ready in plenty of time. There was only one thing to wear.

She pulled on the same evening gown she wore every Christmas. Before, her sartorial restraint had always seemed practical. Now that she would be attending a ball with a gentleman who dressed like a literal fashion plate, her worn, mint-and-white gown looked hopelessly out of style.

It didn't matter. Even if she designed the most stunning lover's lockets Britain had ever seen... Even if the Duke of Nottingvale was so overcome by her vision and artistry that he was moved to personally endorse her creation... Even if Jonathan's business partner didn't bat an eye at paying a complete stranger fifteen percent of profits made on a locket said stranger designed... Even if every item in the catalogue was a runaway success, making them all famous, and wealthier—and England itself, dressier—than ever before...

There would still be no reason to believe she would see Jonathan again after he left Cressmouth.

Angelica could send her designs by post—and indeed, would more likely be working directly with the artisans creating the products than corresponding with them through a third-party investor. There was no reason for anxiety.

Jonathan would only see her in tonight's uninspired gown once. She would get over the embarrassment and forget it ever happened, just as he would forget about her once he moved on to the next town, the next lonely woman he happened to meet.

They would both move on.

None of that stopped her from splashing rose water on her wrists and taking extra time with her hair. Tonight, she parted the front of her hair down the middle, using her fingers to create side-twists to frame her face. The rest of her hair, she pulled twisted back into a chignon, which she decorated with two gold-and-pearl hair combs.

The same ones she hadn't let Jonathan purchase the day they'd met.

When the knock came on her front door, her heart skipped giddily. Although her home shared a common wall with her shop, she was rarely in it except to bathe and sleep. She certainly was unaccustomed to gentleman callers arriving to accompany her to a ball.

Until today.

She rolled her shoulders and lifted her pelisse and bonnet from the rack. Like her gown, there was only one of each. Jonathan had already seen them both any number of times. It was a good thing she wasn't trying to impress him.

Before she could lose her nerve, she flung open the door.

He looked magnificent as always. Shiny black boots. Formal black knee breeches. Perfectly tailored overcoat. Floppy brown hair that fell boyishly over his pale forehead. Strong jaw and firm lips. Sapphire eyes that sparkled wickedly, as though he knew very well how handsome he looked, and enjoyed catching her peeking.

"I brought you something." He pulled his hand out from behind his back.

Angelica stared at the item dangling from his fingers. It was not some romantic trinket, but rather an ordinary beige bonnet she could have sworn came from the same local milliner that had sold her hers. In fact...

"That bonnet looks exactly like mine," she said, her voice tight with suspicion.

"It *is* exactly like yours," he replied cheerfully. "With one big difference: this one is from me." He placed her old bonnet back on the rack and tied the new one beneath her chin. "You hate making clothing decisions. I wanted to give you a gift that didn't add to your worries. There." He stepped back and admired her with satisfaction.

She pressed her fingers to her chest as though her touch could calm her racing heart. It was a perfect gift. Something new to let her know he was thinking of her, without trying to change her in the least. He liked her just as she was, and wanted to be certain she knew it.

He offered his arm.

She held on tighter than necessary, as though

she could imprint the memory of him into each of her fingertips, to keep for later.

He doffed his hat and ducked beneath the brim of her new-old bonnet to steal a quick kiss before escorting her outside and up the snow-packed road to the castle.

They were not alone. Though the air was cold, the atmosphere was festive. Most of Cressmouth regularly turned out for the community's myriad Christmas activities, but the assembly was a particular favorite. Food, drink, music, dancing... and this year, thanks to Noelle, the village's first annual indoor tree decorating. With luck, the custom would catch on.

Volunteers like Jonathan had been out all afternoon, clearing the walking path to the castle. The snow had finally stopped that morning, but it would be days before the roads between neighboring villages were clear enough for travel.

It no longer felt like she and Jonathan were stuck together because of bad weather. It felt more like they'd been drawn together by good luck.

After handing off their outerwear to one of the castle's many attendants, Angelica expected to have to introduce Jonathan to most of the villagers.

She should not have been surprised to discover he'd met all of them already. If the castle pond hadn't frozen over, he probably would have introduced himself to every fish and swan.

The ballroom was stunning. During the renovation period after Mr. Marlowe purchased the castle, he had converted the austere bare-wood ceilings into lush, Elizabethan-style decorative white plaster. Instead of heraldic beasts or family crests, the frieze pattern incorporated Christmastide motifs like sprigs of holly.

The silk-covered walls were of rich emerald green, and decorated with countless bright sconces that complemented the dazzling crystal chandeliers overhead.

Angelica knew from experience that the wooden floor would have been freshly waxed and dusted, but with half of the village already in attendance, all she could see was a sea of sharp gentlemen in formal black suits and waves of beautiful ladies in their best Yuletide gowns.

By the time they made their way up to the ballroom dais where Noelle had stationed an enormous evergreen, it was time for the grand unveiling.

Not that the tree was hidden from view. The boughs were covered in flickering candles as well as tantalizing bags of sweetmeats and other little treats.

Noelle clapped her hands together. The roar of conversations lowered to a soft rumble.

"Thank you so much for coming to Cressmouth's annual grand Yuletide ball. I also want to thank the Skeffington family for providing our beautiful tree, Mr. Bauer for providing countless packages of treats, and Miss Angelica Parker for graciously agreeing to personally design the crowning touches. Even though she had no time to do so, she managed the impossible." Noelle grinned at Angelica.

Angelica grinned back. She'd been skeptical of an indoor tree, but it looked like Noelle was the one who had made a miracle. The festive display was gorgeous.

"Without further ado," Noelle announced, "we present... holly that lasts forever!"

The sound of flutes and clarinets filled the ballroom as ten lads marched through the open doors in pairs, playing a rousing rendition of "The Twelve Days of Christmas."

On the dais, they exchanged their instruments for Angelica's bejeweled gold creations. They displayed the glittering red-berried adornments to the crowd, to oohs and aahs. The lads took turns dragging a wooden stool about to find the perfect tall branch upon which to affix each adornment.

"The tree looks incredible," she whispered to Jonathan.

"Thanks to you," he whispered back. "I hope you're as proud of you as I am."

"Angelica!" called a voice.

It was Luther, her brother.

"I should go," Jonathan said.

"Go? You don't have to," she said with surprise. "The Yuletide ball is for everyone. Don't let my family frighten you away."

"It's not your family." He shifted his weight. "I'm not a great lover of Christmastide. I came because of *you*, not Yuletide. Oh look, there are your nieces. I'll just—"

"One dance," she said. The orchestra was setting bows to their strings. "And then, if you want to run away, you can."

"Scots don't run *away*," he muttered. "I could stay for two dances if I really wanted to."

"Oh? Shall we join my brother and his wife for this country-dance?"

Jonathan's eyes gleamed with mischief. "The question is, will your brother dance with me?"

"There, that's the Christmas spirit," Angelica said with a laugh. "Shall we find out?"

Luther did indeed cut a sharp figure through every pattern of the dance, as Angelica had known he would. Her brother would never allow anything to disrupt his elegant rhythm on the dance floor.

She was rusty, having not practiced since the previous Yuletide. With so many people making merry in front of a tree bearing adornments she'd created with her own hands, Angelica couldn't help but feel joyful.

They danced in tandem with her brother and sister-in-law until the final figure came to a close. The orchestra barely paused between sets.

The next song was a waltz.

It was impossible to feel awkward as Jonathan led her about the floor in graceful, sweeping steps. Angelica forgot about the tree, forgot about her interminable list of things to do, and just gazed up at him gazing back down at her.

It was a good thing he intended to leave her side after this waltz. If they paid each other too much attention, people would start to talk.

And there was no sense letting them talk about something that was never going to happen.

Jonathan might be a brilliant business partner, traveling tirelessly to spread the word, but he was not someone she could rely on for anything more.

He was going to leave. That was how she had hurt her own family. Now she'd learn what it felt like to have it done to her.

She wouldn't join him, even if it were a possibility. She had her own life, her own shop, and more importantly she was mere days away from completing her contract and being able to rejoin her family.

Jonathan's brow creased. "You stopped smiling. You're not thinking about work, are you?"

She shook her head.

He didn't appear convinced.

"I hadn't planned on staying for Nottingvale's house party. Mostly because I don't like Christmas," he admitted. "But I do like *you*. And it will give you an extra week to design your lockets. You don't need to work yourself to the bone. Enjoy your family while they're here."

Yes, she would.

Angelica's mind turned calculating. Christmas was in four days, but one needn't wait until Christmas morning to spread joy. She could share her Yuletide with the one man who needed it most.

"All right," she said. "I'll take tomorrow as a holiday... on one condition."

He lowered his voice. "Very well, I'll spend the whole day kissing you."

She pretended not to hear him. "Part of Christmas is attending church, as you'll see on Sunday when my uncle preaches."

"I didn't agree to go," Jonathan said quickly.

"You also never said you *wouldn't* go, and besides, aren't you my footman?" She linked her arm with his. "The other part of Christmas is community and tradition. Let me share my family with you. They're amusing. We'll give you a Christmas to remember."

His eyes had lost their luster. "I remember Christmas. It was not enjoyable."

"Let me try," she said softly. "That was then. You don't have to promise me the whole day. Can you do two hours? If you're miserable, say the word, and I'll never mention the word Christmas to you again."

At first, she thought he was going to refuse. Say that he was preemptively miserable, just thinking about a jolly afternoon with her family. Perhaps she shouldn't have asked. Perhaps with his past, nothing at all could make the Yuletide season festive.

"All right." He visibly swallowed his objections. "One Christmas to remember."

CHAPTER 10

Jonathan fidgeted in the middle of a blue velvet sofa in the Duke of Nottingvale's empty parlor. He could not believe he'd agreed to spend even a single moment doing festive things. He hated being festive.

But he would agree to almost anything if it meant more time with Angelica.

He leafed absently through his notebook, pausing now and again at one of the many sketches he had made of her working, or lost in thought, or smiling to greet a customer.

His drawings had never held particular meaning before. Idle doodles to pass the time, sketches of someone or something he had no desire to hurry back to. Jonathan was always rushing off to the next thing.

These portraits, however, he suspected would have worn edges in the near future from paging through them whenever he longed for another moment with Angelica.

Even if it meant pretending to enjoy Christmas.

The butler appeared in the parlor doorway. "Caller for you, sir."

He shoved the notebook back into his waist-coat pocket and leapt to his feet. No matter how much Jonathan had begged, Oswald had refused to allow him to stand next to the front door to wait.

"It's Miss Parker?" Of course it was. Hadn't she said she'd come at ten?

"Indeed." Oswald disappeared back to his station.

Jonathan bared his teeth at a looking-glass and ran a hand through his hair. His clothes were the height of fashion—or would be, as soon the *Fit for a Duke* catalogue launched—but his nerves fluttered oddly whenever he knew he was about to see Angelica.

He rushed down the corridor and into the en-tryway to greet her.

She looked beautiful. It was her same pale pink day dress and wheat-colored pelisse, which only made her shine all the brighter.

"Is that my bonnet?" he asked.

"It's *my* bonnet," she replied pertly.

He grinned. Definitely his. She looked stun-ning in it.

What he wanted to do most was whirl her into his arms and kiss her, but if Oswald was scandalized over the idea of sharing his station, witnessing a peck of the lips would no doubt give the poor man a fit of the vapors.

"I have something for you." She held up her closed hand.

Reverently, he unwrapped her fingers.

In the center of her palm was an oval of bright gold, decorated with brilliant red and turquoise stones and engraved with gorgeous looping whorls that reminded him not of the sea, but of the brisk, snow-flecked wind that rustled the hills of evergreens surrounding the castle.

"A lover's locket," he breathed. It was even better than he'd hoped.

"It's not the prototype," she said quickly. She tilted her hand so that the sparkling gold oval fell from her palm to his. "It's for you."

He pinned it to his waistcoat at once, right next to his heart.

"You don't have to wear it." Her lashes lowered. "There isn't even a portrait inside the frame."

A situation easily remedied, though he would wait until later to decide which of his sketches to add to the locket.

"I adore it," he said, his voice huskier than he intended.

Oswald gave a delicate little cough.

Perhaps the man deserved a fit of the vapors.

"Come along." Angelica looped her arm through Jonathan's. "Our chariot awaits."

"Chariot?" he repeated.

"Well, the Cressmouth version." She grinned up at him. "You'll see."

When they stepped out of the door into the chill winter air, a large, bright red sleigh sat at the edge of the street, with a glossy black horse and bright-eyed driver at the ready and a low bench for riders at the rear.

Jonathan had watched the sleighs go by any number of times since his arrival. Tourists used them instead of hackneys. Sleighs were far more reliable in inclement winter weather than anything with axles and wheels. Better yet, they were diverting to ride in, and lent the simple act of traveling down the road an air of adventure and whimsy.

He climbed in after Angelica. "Where are we going?"

"To the park," she replied, brown eyes shining. "The Yuletide festival is underway."

Och. For a brief moment, he forgot about Christmas. But there was no time for his muscles to stiffen with trepidation—the horse was off at a sharp clip, and Angelica's warm curves pressed deliciously into his side.

Because the duke's cottage was only a few hundred yards from the castle, the minutes flew by in a trice. Their sleigh pulled up behind a dozen others, all painted bright red and pulled by exquisite black horses with improbably gleaming coats.

"Courtesy of the Harper stud farm you passed on your way in," Angelica explained. Her glove brushed his. "Ready to meet the rest of my relatives?"

Not in the slightest. The idea terrified him. Which was patently ridiculous.

Jonathan had spent every day for well over a decade meeting strangers and turning them into temporary friends. A task made easier by the knowledge that his success or lack thereof didn't really matter. No matter what sort of impression he made, he'd be gone within a week.

But Angelica's family *did* matter. They mattered because *she* did. Even though he was unlikely to run into them again once he left Cressmouth, he didn't want them to remember him as someone unworthy of Angelica's time.

He desperately wanted them to like him. A situation that all but ensured he would be at his most awkward.

"Where will we meet—" His question was answered before he finished asking.

They were barely out of the sleigh before a dozen children of various heights surrounded them from all angles, followed by an equal number of adults carrying forgotten mittens or cones of paper piled high with roasted chestnuts.

All of them were speaking at once.

"Jump in," Angelica whispered. "It's the only way."

No wonder her quiet little jeweler's shop had seemed eerily silent to her. There were at least four enthusiastic stories being told at once, along with a heated argument over a missing doll, two warring Christmas carols, and some sort of rhyming game involving the complex clapping of hands.

"Family, this is Jonathan." Angelica introduced him to each new face in turn. "My cousin Letitia. If she challenges you to hopscotch, it's a trick. Uncle Maurice, who normally preaches in London but holds a special service in the castle every Christmas. Aunt Octavia, who cooks the most delicious... well, everything, really."

"How can you eat that castle food all year long?" Aunt Octavia fussed at Angelica's pelisse. "No wonder you're so skinny. When I get you back to London—"

"I weigh five pounds more than I did when I left home," Angelica whispered to Jonathan. "But I'd be three stone heavier just from breathing in the aroma from her kitchen. It might be the thing I miss the most about home."

"I thought you missed us the most!" clamored the nieces Jonathan had met previously, a claim that was at once challenged by three other nieces and a small army of nephews.

He repeated everyone's names over and over again in his mind, determined to commit them all to memory. Not just names, but faces. The sensation of having so many people inspecting him all at once was dizzying.

Some of her relatives were smiling.

Some were not.

He didn't blame them. He could only imagine their experiences with those that would judge them based on the color of their skin. The sight of him with their beloved relative must have come as a shock.

His throat tightened. If ever someone had cause to reject him, it was this close-knit family who clearly adored Angelica. In their shoes, he would no doubt feel the same.

What must she have told them?

This is Jonathan MacLean, an overly friendly Scotsman who barged into my shop and plied me with pies until I got used to his canty blether and no longer wanted to shoo him out. He'll be leaving soon enough, though. No need to get used to him.

Jonathan was used to being an outsider. Yet he had never wanted to belong as much as he did in that moment. He wanted them to like him. Wanted to taste the aunt's cooking, wanted to participate in a cutthroat game of hopscotch, wanted to find the missing doll.

But the thought of having all those things was frightening. If he ever *did* belong somewhere, or to someone, leaving would feel like ripping his heart in two.

Missing one person would be torture enough. Missing an entire family... He could not allow himself to get attached.

"Jonathan MacLean, at your service." he began, as he always did, smiling at each one in turn. "Ask me anything. I'm an open book."

The smiling relatives spoke over each other at once.

"Angelica says you're well-traveled. Have you ever seen—"

"Angelica says you're selling fancy clothes from a catalogue. What about—"

"Esther and Florence said you gave them a mountain of biscuits. Did you bring any for us?"

The tension in his shoulders eased. Had he worried about thinking up things to say? Young and old alike peppered him with questions the entire winding path around the castle.

"Angelica says you've been to our neighborhood. Do you know the haberdasher on the corner of—"

"Angelica says you're quite the artist. Can you draw—"

"Where's your tartan? Do you play the bagpipes?"

Jonathan answered each question as thoroughly and entertainingly as possible, providing detail and making exaggerated faces and funny voices to go along with each story.

By the time they emerged from the other side of the evergreens, what had started as somewhat of an interrogation was now a hotchpotch of teasing and banter across all parties. No wonder Angelica had missed being in the midst of such loving chaos. Jonathan had never experienced anything like it.

Before he knew what was happening, he was seated amongst a row of nieces and nephews atop tiny, precarious, flat wooden sleds at the top of a hill.

Angelica grinned at him. "Off you go, vagabond!"

She gave his shoulder a little push, and his sled went flying down the icy-slick slope. Luckily, the children's shrieks drowned out his own.

"Again!" they cried after they tumbled into an inglorious heap at the bottom. "Let's do it again!"

"My heart..." Jonathan clutched at his lapel. "I think it's a triple apoplexy..."

"Last one up to the top has to buy chestnuts for everyone else," one of the lads called as he scrambled up the hill.

Jonathan couldn't be expected to let *that* stand. He grabbed the ropes to a few sleds and scooped up the smallest little girl, then charged up the hill to be first in line to purchase chestnuts.

Somewhere between the snowball fight and the fifth round of hot chocolate, he realized the two hours of Yuletide activities he'd begrudgingly promised to tolerate had turned into an entire day full of merriment and laughter. His lips were chapped and his back was sore and his face hurt from all the smiling.

"Admit it," Angelica said as she pulled him onto the frozen pond in rented skates. "My family is utterly mad."

"I have never had a better day in all my life," he confessed.

"In that case..." She spun in a half-circle so that she was facing him. She joined their gloved hands together so she could pull him along with her as she skated backward around the edge of the pond. "Come over to my house after Uncle's

Christmas sermon. He'll destroy you at whist while my aunts and I cook dinner."

As much as he yearned to take part in a family meal, Jonathan had purposefully neglected to agree to the church service. He'd planned to spend Christmas locked alone in his guest chamber.

"I'm sorry." Her smile faltered. "I shouldn't ask you to do so much."

"I'll be there," he blurted out.

What on earth was he saying?

She grinned at him as she guided him over the ice. "It will be the best Christmas dinner you've ever had. Or at least, the most memorable."

"It'll be the only one I've ever had," he mumbled. "Scots don't make a big fuss for the Yuletide, and even if they did… For me, there's never been any cause to celebrate."

She stared at him as though he'd accidentally spoken in Gaelic. "No reason to celebrate *Christmas?*"

His throat grew thick.

"It happens to be my birthday, as well." He was the gift that had ruined lives. "My father was gone long before my birth. Mother believed he would have married her, had she not embarrassed him by becoming pregnant before they could announce the wedding."

Angelica's eyes flashed. "I doubt she managed that feat all on her own."

"He was never going to marry her," Jonathan agreed. "She was poor and expendable. He was a laird and important. He was already promised to another bride, whose land would double his own."

Instead, all his mother got was Jonathan.

"The laird sounds dreadful," Angelica said flatly.

He shrugged. "So I presume."

"You never met him?" she asked in surprise. "It sounded like you knew who he was."

"Aye, *I* knew who *he* was," Jonathan agreed. "He was the man who sent my mother into a melancholy from which she never recovered. His man of business was concerned about quashing inconvenient gossip that might impede the wedding. A trust was created in my name to appease any hurt feelings."

It had done the opposite. He was a problem neither of his parents had wanted.

Most of their money was spent on laudanum to dull her pain. Jonathan was left to raise himself, with no choice but to watch his mother's slow, inevitable decline, courtesy of his own inheritance. The money was cursed, and perhaps so was he. If he hadn't been born, if there'd been no inheritance, she would still be alive.

He had lived with that knowledge every day since.

Mother had never been loving, but Yuletide was the worst. She disappeared completely into her laudanum every December and didn't emerge until January.

For Jonathan, there was no escape at all. He

was too young to live on his own. Until the day the choice was taken from him. The Christmas his mother died, the trust became Jonathan's. There was only one thing to do.

"I was a problem paid to disappear," he said. "When my mother lost her battle with laudanum, I lost my mother. So I left and never looked back. Not at that place or anywhere else."

It had taken years after her death for Jonathan to accept that although his conception had caused his mother's melancholy, Jonathan's existence was not solely to blame. It was the laird who had provided the cursed inheritance, the laird who had lain with an innocent girl with no intention to marry her.

The laird had destroyed her just as surely as the laudanum.

Happy Christmas.

"You used your inheritance to start a successful investing operation?" Angelica asked.

"I did not." Each syllable was chipped ice. "I give my sire's money away freely to anyone who will take it. I forged my own way however I could. No task too menial; no pay too small. I took risks. I got better at choosing them. I invested in myself, and then in others."

People who were unseen. People whom no one believed in. People who needed someone to say, *I see you. You have value. You're important to the world.*

"And you never met him?"

"I did try once." The words came out scratchy.

"I didn't expect him to recognize my face, but it was worse than that. He didn't remember my name, or that I had ever existed."

That was the day Jonathan had decided *everyone* would know his name. He would become so important and so successful that his father would not be able to avoid hearing *Jonathan MacLean this*, and *Jonathan MacLean that*, from every angle.

He would eclipse his father's fame, without aid of a title, without the trust the laird had set up and forgotten, just like he'd forgotten the son he never wanted and hoped would disappear.

"It's human to feel hurt," Angelica said softly. "Even if you wish others didn't have the power to hurt you."

How he *hated* that his father still wielded that much power over his life.

The man had never known him. Jonathan had been disavowed whilst still in the womb. His birth, proof of failure. The reason he had lost his mother, on a day just like today.

"That's why I don't like Christmas," he said, his words thick. "There's naught to celebrate."

Not yet, anyway. The day he was finally richer and more successful than his father, he would raise his fist to the sky in satisfaction.

Until then, he would just keep moving.

CHAPTER 11

The next morning, Jonathan did not go straight to Angelica's jeweler's shop, as had become their delightful custom. Just as he was tying his cravat, a handsome coach-and-four bearing an extravagant family crest pulled to a halt in front of the cottage.

The Duke of Nottingvale had arrived. The English aristocrat whose public endorsement would ensure Fit for a Duke's commercial success. The wealthy nob whose initial investment into the fledgling company would finance materials, wages, tens of thousands of catalogues, and operating expenses for up to a full year. The influential man whose popularity and handsomeness was the bedrock upon which Jonathan's bright future rested.

He had never been more disappointed to see a carriage in his life.

Nottingvale's arrival precipitated Jonathan's

departure. Once the presentation was over and the contract signed, it would be time to move on.

Even if it hadn't been for his visceral aversion to Christmas, which was two days hence, Jonathan's place was on the road.

Nottingvale's contributions were his name and his money. Calvin's contribution was his genius with fashion. Jonathan's contributions were his feet and his mouth. He was to spread the word far and wide. The sooner he started, the quicker the path to success.

Of course, all that would happen once Calvin arrived. He had Jonathan's sketches for the catalogue as well as prototypes of the latest designs.

The duke would be eager to move forward with the plans. The idea was excellent and Calvin's artistry undeniable. Nottingvale was *lucky* to be considered as a founding investor. The duke was no fool.

Jonathan might be.

He should be preparing for what might be the most pivotal meeting of his life, not mooning out of the window because he'd rather be reading geology texts aloud on a hard wooden stool at Angelica's counter than making small talk in a duke's sumptuous parlor.

Nottingvale's retinue was breathtakingly efficient. In no time at all, the duke's trunks were carried inside, the duke himself trimmed and cleaned and starched, and Jonathan trundled into the dining room to join him for nuncheon.

He'd forgotten about the dining room. For the

past fortnight, he'd taken almost every meal with Angelica.

The duke's dining room could seat two dozen. It seemed improbably big and impossibly lonely. Perhaps that was the real reason Nottingvale hosted an annual party. He couldn't bear sitting at the head of that enormous mahogany table all alone.

That was the best part about not having a home, Jonathan decided. One never had to confront one's loneliness.

Just when he began to despair of Calvin ever arriving, a significantly less grand carriage pulled up before the cottage, and the most talented tailor in the world leapt out.

"We'll have to be quick," said the duke. "Guests could arrive at any moment."

"Of course," Jonathan said. "We just need a moment."

A moment in which there would be no rehearsing, which was bound to worry nervous Calvin. There would also be no time to sort through the sketches and paint the best ones to look like fashion plates. Nottingvale would have to use his imagination—or trust in theirs.

Jonathan met Calvin at the door and ushered him into the parlor, where they worked quickly to set up Calvin's life-sized manikin with the latest fashions Calvin had designed. Jonathan's dream of making his fortune on his own was finally within his grasp. Without his father's coin.

Only then would he be able to think about making a home.

The presentation *almost* went off without a hitch, except for the part where the duke's sister crashed the meeting, which only caused the duke to even more stubbornly insist in taking part in the venture. He agreed to Angelica's involvement at once, as well as to only using suppliers with no involvement in the slave trade, even if it meant higher prices for materials like cotton.

"The designs are magnificent. Let's start production on the catalogues." The duke turned to Jonathan. "How soon can you start putting them into people's hands?"

"Tomorrow," Jonathan said automatically. He could have said *today*, but he wasn't leaving Cressmouth without seeing Angelica one last time.

The duke laughed. "Even if I poach the castle's printing press, tomorrow is Christmas Eve. I doubt we can start production in earnest until Twelfth Night. You're not leaving before then, are you?"

Twelve days of constant Yuletide under one roof. Twelve days of partiers, partying. Tra-la-la, all day long. Happy Christmas this, and Merry Christmas that.

Nothing could entice Jonathan less.

He wouldn't think about that now. He would think about telling Angelica the good news about her involvement with the project. Politely, he took his leave from Calvin and the duke.

And soon, he must take his leave from Angelica.

His chest seized at the thought. Jonathan flung out a hand to the wall for balance. Never see her again. Never come back, because every moment *here* was a moment he wasn't out *there* spreading the word.

Never see each other again.

The idea was insupportable. Unfathomable. He couldn't breathe at the sudden sense of loss. He loved her too much to—

God help him. Of all the untimely, foolish complications, Jonathan had fallen in *love*.

He raked trembling fingers through his hair. He was in love. Did it change anything? Or ought he now to be even more determined to give this project every beat of his heart, knowing it would help Angelica reap all the success she deserved?

Perhaps he was looking at this backward. His heart lightened. *He* needed to travel as far and wide as possible, but he didn't need to do it alone.

Angelica had said herself that her seven-year contract expired on Christmas. Only two days remained. Come Sunday, she wouldn't be tethered to Cressmouth anymore. She could come *with* him. Perhaps not every second of every day for the rest of their lives—she was a jeweler, and would want to spend some time in her shop creating jewelry—but their paths could intersect.

Instead of Jonathan wandering the world alone, they could build their future together.

It was past ten when Angelica awoke the next morning, but she did not rush into her shop to prepare for business. It was Christmas Eve. She would spend the next two full days with her friends and family and, if he wished to join them, with Jonathan.

He had helped her to realize that she worked better and faster when she took time for herself, to rest and make merry. Waiting until the work was done was a mirage—the work would never be done. She had to take time for the things that mattered. Her family, Jonathan, and herself.

Closing her eyes again, she stretched her limbs out like a starfish, reveling in the freedom of not having to do anything at all. Not only had she delivered the last of the outstanding jewelry orders last night, today marked the last day in her seven-year contract with Mr. Marlowe.

At midnight tonight, the shop would be hers.

Better yet, her *life* would be hers. Visits with

her family would no longer be limited to Yuletide. She could travel to London whenever she pleased. She would spend the busiest months here in Cressmouth, of course, but the thought of seeing Vauxhall fireworks again, of being able to celebrate the births of nieces and nephews, of enjoying her aunts' cooking... it was almost too wonderful to bear.

She rolled out of bed to attend to her morning ablutions, then applied skin creams and arranged her hair without any of the usual haste. Her spirits were high. Today, the sweetmeats adorning the castle tree weren't just for decoration—children would be allowed to retrieve the little bags and consume the treats inside.

Perhaps she could talk Jonathan into an entire day of pleasure-taking. *Twelfth Night* was to be performed in the amphitheatre this afternoon, then a tour of the castle grounds, followed by another assembly with music and dancing.

Her skin warmed at the memory of being in his arms. Waltzing together in the castle ballroom. Holding hands as they skated across the frozen pond. Her smile faltered. That conversation had been far less merry.

No wonder he hadn't pressed her when she'd reiterated she would not lie with a man she wasn't married to. Because of his mother, Jonathan likely felt the same way. He would not treat such an act casually.

Despite his attempts to appear flippant and carefree, she doubted there was much he did take lightly. Her heart ached at the thought that Christmas meant sorrow to him, instead of happiness. She wished she could bring him joy.

No—she wished he could find his *own* joy.

Cressmouth had welcomed Jonathan from the start. She doubted there was a single soul he hadn't bowed to and won over with charm and the shameless allure of free biscuits.

Her relatives weren't as easy to win, but spending the day with Jonathan had illustrated to them the sort of man he was. She was lucky to have a large, loving family. Her nieces and nephews would have no problem considering him an honorary uncle. He was the opposite of what Luther had imagined for his sister, but even he had grudgingly admitted Jonathan seemed all right.

It would all be perfect, except for two tiny details:

She loved him.

He was going to leave.

Angelica put the kettle on to give herself something to do with her hands. Jonathan had been frank about his temporariness from the moment they'd first met. She could not claim abandonment or betrayal.

At the time, it had been what she liked best about their arrangement: that it would end. She'd be through with him, she'd have finished her contract, and life would be a bright open road.

But it was *Jonathan* who would be moving on, not her. Out of sight, out of mind. How long would it take him to forget her? There was no sense admitting her heart had got tangled up. It wouldn't make a difference. She had her future planned out, and so did he.

A knock sounded on the front door. Angelica set down her tea and all but ran to answer it.

Jonathan.

Her heart beat triple-time, despite all her best intentions. Just the sight of him brought a smile to her face and a lightness to her limbs.

Even if he was carrying a... What on earth was he carrying?

She shut the door behind him. "What—"

Jonathan swept into her parlor with a life-size wicker manikin in his arms. Before she could get out the whole question, he stood the manikin to one side and claimed her mouth with a kiss.

She wrapped her arms about his neck and kissed him back, imbuing their embrace with the love she dare not admit to. Their first Christmas together would be their last.

When he finally broke their kiss, Jonathan made a dramatic gesture toward the wicker man.

"This," he announced, "is Duke. I bought him from Calvin for ten quid."

"You did?" she said faintly. "Why?"

He waved his fingers. "Calvin has others back home in his workshop. This one was created to the Duke of Nottingvale's measurements so that all the prototypes would be ready to wear."

"Fit for a Duke," she said slowly. "A *real* duke."

"The spit and image." Jonathan patted the

manikin's wicker shoulder. "We won't hold it against him."

"But... why is it *here?*"

"Nottingvale agreed to everything! He'll start printing the catalogues as soon as reasonable. He and Calvin will work out where to source materials for the apparel and who to employ for expedient production, and I will be off spreading the good word. I have news about your percentage, by the way."

"They wouldn't agree to fifteen percent?"

"You'll have to make do with twenty. It was the best I could do." He grinned at her.

Her heart skipped, then stuttered even faster.

"Duke is here to keep you company when I cannot," he continued. "If you don't like him, I'm told he can be excellent kindling for one's fire. Very practical, this beast."

"When you... cannot?" she stammered. "Does that mean you'll be back sometime?"

"What if I said many times?" His gaze held hers. "Would that be all right?"

Her breath caught. "I... You..."

"I'll primarily be traveling," he warned. "Perhaps fifty weeks out of the year. But Nottingvale has made the very good point that people are otherwise engaged over the Yuletide, and should not be harassed by nagging salesmen decked in extremely fashionable ensembles. Which would give me a fortnight to spend with you."

Her exhilaration faded.

"You want to spend every Christmas with me," she said warily, "and *only* Christmas?"

"I'm willing to spend Christmas *here*," he corrected. "And only Christmas. But the rest of the time, you can travel with me! The factory will produce all the lockets based on your designs. You won't need to lift a finger. Now that you're not anchored to this village anymore, there's no reason to be in it at all!"

She gaped at him. He surely couldn't mean…

"No reason," she repeated carefully, "except the fact that I've dedicated seven years of my life to becoming part of a community, establishing my reputation, and making my store a stop worth seeing on every tourist's visit to Cressmouth. I sacrificed precious years with my family because I *want* this. I *am* a jeweler. I *like* my work. My shop is finally mine, and you want me to give it up for… grueling hackney rides around England?"

"Not *all* of the time," he said, as though she weren't quite catching on. "I assumed you'd want to be here *sometimes*, which is why I brought Duke to accompany you when I cannot. Och, I forgot the most important bit. I'm not asking you to live in sin with an itinerant salesman. I'm asking you to be my wife."

She stared at him. "You're asking me to accept a model replica of my neighbor instead of a flesh-and-blood husband?"

"I *said*—" The words came out with exaggerated patience. "—that you could come *with* me. It cannot be my fault if you choose to stay here."

She couldn't believe what she was hearing. "You're not proposing marriage. You're proposing I give up everything I worked for and everyone I love, or live without my husband."

"I'd come for Christmases," he reminded her.

"That sounds *reasonable* to you?" she blurted out. "I don't want a husband for only twelve days of the year. That's not a wife; it's a *holiday*. I'm worth more."

"I'm trying to give you what you're worth. The only way I can provide for you is to—"

"I didn't ask you to provide for me. *I* provide for me. When I marry, it will be to a man, not to a coin purse." She crossed her arms to hide her shaking hands. "Your excuse is hogwash anyway. If the only thing missing from our union was money, don't you have a bank account that could solve your troubles?"

"No," he said flatly. "I'm not spending the laird's blood money on me. I'll earn my way on my own or not at all. I have my own account, with coin *I've* earned. My life shall be a success in spite of my father, not because of him."

"Then you've given it all away? Every farthing from the trust?"

He sighed. "Barely a dent, no matter how hard I try. It keeps earning interest."

"So, you *could* have a home, and choose not to. You could pay someone *else* to travel about England delivering catalogues. You could probably employ a team to deliver in every shire."

"I told you," he said. "My success shall come from *my* efforts to stand out, not the money my father spent to hide me away. I'd sooner live under a bridge than accept gold as a substitute for a father."

"But you expect me to accept a wicker manikin instead of a husband?" Her laugh felt like broken glass. "Goodbye, Jonathan. Marriage means making a home, not providing a posting house. If you're just passing through... Do us both a favor, and stay gone."

CHAPTER 13

Jonathan had never looked forward to Christmas Day, and this one was already miserable. The house was positively brimming with revelers.

They'd started the night before—carols and puddings and charades and spiced wine. After being up all night making merry, they somehow managed to be merry *all over again*. He'd lost count of the number of people who'd knocked on his door offering well-wishes or invitations to join them for roast goose or rousing parlor games.

Jonathan was *not* going in that parlor.

There was mistletoe in there.

Last night, the only woman he had any desire to kiss had brushed him off as efficiently as a maid sweeping unwanted debris from the front step.

Stay gone, she'd said. Would that he could!

But it was the wretched day known as Christmas, in a tiny village *also* known as Christmas, which meant there wasn't a single hack to be had. He could get a sleigh ride to the castle if he wanted to nauseate himself with even more music and dancing, but not a single soul could be convinced to drag him far away at any price.

His head ached. So did his heart.

He should be grateful Angelica was clever enough to end things now, rather than wait until resentment ate them alive and the only ties binding them were for business. He should be *glad*. He should be *relieved*.

Besides, what ties would bind them? Angelica hadn't seemed particularly tempted by any part of his offer. It was a douse of cold water. Jonathan had got used to being the hero. To coming along and saving the day.

But Angelica didn't need saving.

Nor did she need him.

Jonathan glared out his window at the drifting snow. He would show her. As soon as he had the catalogues, he would hire a hack and journey to every corner of England until Fit for a Duke was more popular than fresh bread. She would earn fistfuls of money from his efforts. He wouldn't stop until her name was on everyone's lips. Until he finally proved himself worthy of her.

Once *she* was as rich as Croesus, well, *then* they could decide what to do, couldn't they? His father's bribe money wouldn't matter anymore. Once Jonathan and Angelica both were independently wealthy on their own merits...

How long would that take? How much was enough? Even if he managed to earn it, would she still want him by then? Was staying out of her life the best plan?

A knock came on Jonathan's door.

He ignored it.

The door swung open anyway.

Calvin strode inside and handed Jonathan a mug of steaming chocolate. "Happy Christmas."

"Not you, too," Jonathan muttered.

"The others are about to play a game of—"

"No."

"Should I have brought Scotch whisky instead of chocolate?"

Jonathan sniffed the warm contents of the mug. It smelled delicious, damn it. Hot and sweet. The steam banished the chill from the air.

"I'll suffer through," he muttered.

Calvin eased onto the dressing-stool uninvited. "I thought you hated being stuck inside a room."

"I do. There's no hack to be had or I'd be gone." Jonathan glared at him. "I don't know how you can prefer to lock yourself in your house for months on end, sewing clothes."

"I don't know how you can prefer not to *have* a house," Calvin countered, unruffled.

"What's the point?" Jonathan crossed one boot over the other. "A house doesn't make a home."

"Are you an expert on the subject?" Calvin's brows rose. "Tell me, what makes a home?"

Jonathan feigned deep interest in his chocolate rather than respond.

Very well, he wasn't feigning. This was excellent chocolate.

"Home isn't necessarily a building," Calvin said, as though Jonathan were at all interested in conversing with him. "It can be a person. Home isn't what holds you back. It's the thing you hate to leave."

"I *like* to travel." Perhaps *like* wasn't the right word. He was compelled to travel. It was a race, from the past to the future. "The world is big. I don't want to miss anything."

"Maybe all you're missing," Calvin said, "is slowing down."

Jonathan did his best to incinerate him with the force of his glare.

It might have worked better if he wasn't peeking out over a mug of hot chocolate.

Calvin was unperturbed. He narrowed his eyes in consideration. "I would think being constantly on the move means you can never get close to anyone."

"I wish *you* were far away," Jonathan muttered.

"You can never enjoy your achievements because you're always on the hunt for the next one," Calvin continued. "You never rest, or take a moment for introspection."

"I hate being alone with my thoughts,"

Jonathan said. "That's why I tell people to ask me anything. I'd rather think about their thoughts than mine."

"I love being alone," Calvin said.

Jonathan tilted his head. That was a strange argument.

"But I'll like having a wife even better," Calvin finished. He was recently betrothed.

"Humph." Jonathan snorted. He wasn't jealous.

He was very jealous.

If only the things he wanted weren't mutually exclusive! He adored exploring new places and having adventures. But he did yearn for somewhere to call his home. Someone to miss him when he was gone. Someone to come home *to*.

No... not "someone" in general.

Angelica in specific.

He longed for her more than he'd ever longed for anything. With her, everything was better. He hadn't minded being cooped up in a tiny jeweler's shop. He'd looked forward to it. Rushed over at first light. Schemed how best to stay all day.

Just to have one more moment with her.

"I've seen how you spend money," Calvin said hesitantly. "If you're now in a tight spot, just let me know and I'll—"

"Good God, no," Jonathan interrupted.

When he had told Angelica his history, he hadn't thought of it in the context of other people's experiences, including her own. Jonathan was the son of a laird, boo-hoo. Jonathan's father forced a very large amount of money upon him, boo-hoo.

Nobody could guess the circumstances of his birth by looking at him. Being the bastard of a laird made Jonathan rich, not poor. He was accepted into more places, not fewer. He was actively choosing not to utilize his many advantages.

How had she managed not to box his ears?

If he hated the money so much, he could give it all to charity. Or to abolitionists. Or to orphanages. Was it really such a cross to bear?

As female and Black, Angelica had dealt with far worse disadvantages, and she wasn't spending her Christmas sobbing into a mug of hot chocolate. She was a clever, talented, joyful success, with a delightful, loving, joyful family. She had not one home, but two.

And he had asked her to give both up in favor of peddling waistcoats and fancy breeches.

All because of his father.

Jonathan had let his entire world be upset by one person discounting him. He glowered at his chocolate. Although he gave the trust money away, his actions bought the appreciation and approval his father had never given him.

The time had come to move on. The only person who should hold the reins of his life was himself.

"I've never found a place I felt I belonged to," he admitted.

Calvin looked at him in disbelief. "*Nowhere*

you've traveled through might possibly do? Have you considered that it might be up to *you* to make a place your home, rather than expect the place to do it for you?"

Jonathan did not dignify this excellent rejoinder with a reply.

The truth was, he'd been searching for belonging. From the moment of his conception, all the places he'd seen and all the people he'd met had let him leave without complaint. He wanted someone to stop him.

It had never happened.

"Whatever you're thinking," Calvin said. "Turn it around."

Jonathan scowled at him. What an absolutely insufferable prig.

Who might be right.

Maybe Angelica didn't want to have to *ask* Jonathan to stay. Maybe she wanted *him* to want to.

To choose *her*.

Instead, Jonathan's grand plan had been... to leave her behind. To expect coin to be enough, just like his father had done to Jonathan and his mother.

"Ah," said Calvin. "You're wearing an I've-been-an-idiot expression. A common affliction among those who are the root of their own problems."

"I've walked away from the only place that felt like home," Jonathan admitted. "The only *person* that felt like home."

"'Idiot' may not be strong enough of a word." Calvin's expression was sympathetic. "I know what that feels like."

Jonathan took a shaky breath. "The idea of needing one particular, irreplaceable person is terrifying."

"And when people are frightened," Calvin said, "they run away."

Scots don't run, Jonathan had told Angelica. And then did the opposite.

"I love her," he said. "I love her so much I can't tell if I'm coming or going."

"You should decide," Calvin suggested. "I feel that's the crux of the matter."

Jonathan cleared his throat. "What if I don't spend every moment of the next year hawking our catalogues from door to door?"

"I hope you realize," said Calvin, "I will not be spending every moment of even the next month sewing on buttons or devising new ways to fold neckcloths. We're all allowed time to ourselves. You just have to decide what you want to do with yours."

There was naught to figure out. Jonathan already knew the answer.

He wanted Angelica.

She had heard every thought he'd ever had on why he was a rolling stone whom no one place could tempt to stay. He'd been wrong. The question was how to convince her he wanted to put things right.

"How can I slow down, when I must place a catalogue into every future customer's hand?"

"What if you didn't?" Calvin suggested.

"Then how would we—" But an idea was already forming. He sat up straight. "Haberdashers."

"Haberdashers?" Calvin repeated politely.

"Instead of printing and delivering catalogues to individual customers, we could provide them to each town's local shops instead. Our customers would visit the shops to place their orders, which would increase the shopkeepers' business, too. We could even offer them a commission."

"Don't you dare name the number," Calvin warned. "I will discuss an appropriate commission with Nottingvale."

Jonathan was happy to hand over the finer details. He had suddenly freed entire future months of his life. There were far fewer haberdashers than individual customers. Making the rounds would take time, but far less than he had feared.

"I suppose Fit for a Duke must have a headquarters." If it was here in Cressmouth...

"London," Calvin said, as though it were the most obvious thing in the world. Jonathan supposed it was. "Besides being the center of the British postal system, I live there, Nottingvale spends the majority of his time there, all the most influential dandies and designers are there..."

None of that signified.

Jonathan set down his mug of chocolate. He didn't need a pretext to stay. He had a reason: Angelica. She was more than enough.

That was, if she'd give him a second chance.

CHAPTER 14

*A*ngelica cast an emotional eye about her parlor. It was *hers* now. Truly hers.

Today was Christmas in every sense of the word. She had all the things she'd worked so hard for. A shop, in her name. A home she owned outright. Recognition for her skill. A marvelous new business opportunity.

She flung her arms out wide and spun in a circle. She was *free* from her contract with Mr. Marlowe.

Without the specter of seven years' worth of high rents hanging over her, she could now share her savings with her family; send home funds as often as she liked. Not just money—Angelica could go *herself*. She could embrace them, kiss their cheeks, talk with them, laugh with them, even when it wasn't Christmas.

Could there be a better gift than family?

Soon, they would all meet back here after the church service to celebrate. The Yule log was in the fireplace, and festive boughs decorated with ribbons were placed strategically throughout her home. In a few hours, the cozy interior would overflow with conversation and love.

She'd prepared as much food as possible in advance, so that the evening could be spent with each other, rather than in the kitchen. The others had gone to claim the best pew in the chapel for Uncle Maurice's sermon. They were an hour early, but one could not be too careful about such things.

Angelica was glad she hadn't mentioned Jonathan would be joining them for their Christmas meal. She didn't want to have to explain his absence.

Not that she would be saved from questions. No doubt half her family would chide her for *not* having invited him.

Once he was gone for good—if he wasn't already—she could also look forward to questions from the rest of the village. Had she heard from Jonathan? What news did she have? When would he be back? *No. None. Never.*

It was almost enough to make her want to stay home this time.

But that wasn't a choice, and Angelica wasn't the sort who cowered. She would field uncomfortable questions with grace, and go about her life with her head held high.

No matter how she felt inside.

The wicker duke stood in a corner of her bedchamber. After spending a long night with its blank face watching over her in silence, she could state unequivocally that its presence was nothing at all like being with Jonathan. Angelica didn't have the heart to toss it into a fire, but she might make a donation to the local haberdasher in the morning.

She hurried down the stairs and into her jeweler's shop to ensure the sign was turned to CLOSED.

A figure stood outside, gloved hands tucked against his sides and his hat pulled low to block out the wind.

Her lungs caught, even though it wasn't Jonathan.

It was her brother Luther.

She unlocked the shop door and cracked it open just far enough to peek outside. "Why in heaven's name are you standing outside in the cold?"

"Waiting for you," he said, teeth chattering. "Thought we could walk to church together."

Her heart warmed. "That's a lovely idea. One moment, whilst I grab my coat."

As her hand reflexively moved to close the door, Angelica paused. What was she doing? Leaving her brother out in freezing weather because of her personal policy to refuse him entrance into her shop? He wasn't here to mock her achievements, or to look around and list all the ways he would have done things better.

And even if he was... it was Christmas. Love was stronger than pride.

She pulled open the door. "Don't just stand there."

His eyes widened. "I can come in?"

She stepped aside, as though her heart weren't knocking against her ribs. The last time they'd both been in the same jeweler's shop, they'd found themselves in yet another shouting match.

Luther had said their father was right to leave the shop to him, and him alone. He was older. He knew best. He didn't need a quarrelsome baby sister underfoot.

Months later, Angelica had informed him that he needn't worry about her being in the way. She'd been offered her own shop, elsewhere. After seven years, the rewards would be even greater.

Luther had laughed, said she wouldn't last seven days.

And now he was stepping across her threshold.

He glanced about in wonder. "Your shop is..."

Small? Tidy? Insignificant?

"...impressive," he finished. His gaze went to the window display. "You designed all of these?"

She nodded, not trusting her voice. Those were the most inexpensive trinkets. Her most expensive, intricate work was locked away until after Christmas when her shop reopened. If Luther judged her based solely on her cheapest product—

"Your technique has matured, but I recognize your style." He stepped from one piece to another, slowly, deliberately, as if savoring precious artifacts in a museum exhibition. "I especially liked the leaves on your holly adornments. Your *repoussé* is second to none."

Had he just... complimented her? Had her brother *ever* complimented her artistry before?

"You've always been second to none." He turned to face her. "And I've always been jealous of my little sister's talent. I've finally grown up enough to admit it."

"*I've* always been jealous," she admitted. "You got everything I ever wanted, and you didn't even have to try."

"Didn't have to *try?*" He let out a choking laugh. "I barely saw my own bedchamber, from spending every hour of every day in the shop, hunched over the work bench, trying again and again to halfway execute techniques that came to you naturally."

"Then why did Father bequeath the shop to you instead of me?" Her nails dug into her palms. "Why didn't he leave it to both of us equally?"

"Because we're not equal, Angel." Luther gave a soft chuckle. "Father saw that I put in the time, that I would dedicate my life to the shop if need be. And he saw you were meant for greater things."

Her throat tightened. "But you... You were so dreadful about me moving to Cressmouth..."

"I envied you." His eyes held hers. "But the real reason I didn't want you to go was because you're my sister. I was afraid if you left, I'd never get you back. That you'd be lost to me forever."

Her eyes pricked with heat.

"I'm not lost, big brother." She stepped closer. "I'm right here."

He wrapped her in a tight embrace. "Do you forgive an old fool?"

"Do you forgive a younger and prettier one?" she mumbled into his lapel.

Luther laughed and let her go. "I did improve, you know. You should see the shop now. This spring, I may have to employ even more nieces and nephews."

"That's wonderful." A lightness filled her. "And I *will* be able to see it. As of today, I'm free to go where I please."

He stepped back in surprise. "You'd leave Cressmouth?"

"Only for a holiday," she admitted. "The first one I'll take will be to come and see you."

He cocked a brow. "Will you be arriving on the arm of a certain Scotsman?"

Her joy dimmed.

"No." She pulled her muffler off the rack and wrapped it about her head and neck methodically. "I wouldn't depend on that."

Her brother frowned. "Did something happen?"

She shoved her arms into the sleeves of her pelisse. "He wanted me to give up everything I care about or worked hard for, to go traveling from town to town with him. To have no home or shop or family or stability."

"And he became enraged when you pointed out that was the last thing you'd ever want to do?" Luther guessed.

"Not at all." She fastened her buttons. "He said it was no problem for me to stay here. He'd visit me every Christmas, just like you do."

Luther narrowed his eyes. "Should I punch him?"

"You should not punch him." She looped her arm through her brother's. "You won't see him again, anyway. He never returns to the same place twice."

"But you said he *would* have. For you." Luther pushed open the door. "What did he say when you proposed a more reasonable compromise?"

The icy wind smacked Angelica in the face.

"Er," she said.

Had she proposed a reasonable compromise? Or had her anger and hurt feelings caused her to turn him away, without even attempting to fight for the love blossoming between them?

"I see," Luther said. "Well, I'm certain you know best."

"I really don't," she mumbled. "I'm a disaster."

"I know," he assured her. "I was just being supportive."

She elbowed him in the side.

"You might be the better craftsman," he said, "but after nine years of marriage, I know a thing or two about love."

"Who said anything about love?" she muttered.

"Your face did." He slanted her a look. "When you love someone, you find a way to be together."

Her throat prickled. "He's already gone."

Because she'd told him to leave.

Because he'd tossed off two ridiculous options, and she hadn't suggested any.

"Is he?" Luther let go of her arm.

Angelica glanced in the direction he indicated.

There, in the castle's open doorway, was Jonathan.

Her thoughts muddled.

"He's not here for me," she babbled. "I'd invited him to church and to dinner, and he probably felt honor-bound to come..."

"Uh-huh." Luther took an exaggerated step aside. "Nothing to do with you at all."

She couldn't see Jonathan's face.

His body was silhouetted by the warm light spilling from the castle. It was exactly like that first moment she'd glanced up from her work to discover a friendly Scot in her shop. Back then, she had thought nothing of yet another tourist passing through. But they were no longer strangers. Now when he left, he would take a piece of her soul with him.

Heart pounding, she closed the distance between them.

The lover's locket she'd given him was affixed to his left lapel. It hung open. The brooch was no longer empty. Her own eye gazed out at her. Sketched with pen; painted with watercolor. A bold pronouncement pinned to his chest that his heart was spoken for.

It belonged to her.

"I'm sorry I let you down," he said, before she could say the same. "I've been so used to my life being a certain way that I failed to envision what a new way would look like. What it *should* look like." He took a deep breath. "I'll stop."

She frowned. "Stop what?"

"Everything. I'll stop running, I'll stop traveling, I'll stop..." He gestured helplessly. "I'll stop being afraid. Or at least, I won't let fear stop *me*. I love you, Angelica. No place would ever be home without you in it."

She took a breath. Compromise. Love was worth it. "You adore travel just as much as I adore crafting jewelry. I didn't want you to stop being *you*. I wanted us to be *us*. For more than twelve days a year."

He touched her cheek. "I may not have a house to offer you, but I do have my heart, my soul, and my life. Those are the things I want to share with you forever. Wherever 'forever' happens to be."

She leaned her cheek into his warm palm and gazed up at him with all the love in her heart. "Don't try to please me. Tell me what *you* need. We'll find a way."

"I need you," he said without hesitation, then paused. "And to travel. It's part of me. I'd like it to be a part of us. Something we do together. Not always—you need your shop, too. But sometimes."

"What if we stayed here during the winter season, and took frequent trips to London to visit my family? *Our* family," she quickly corrected herself. "They'll be yours, now, too."

"I'd like that," he said softly. "What if you came with me sometimes, on journeys to deliver catalogues or whatever future investments might hold?"

"I would adore that." An even better idea occurred to her. "What if we took the long way home on those trips, making sure to visit places that are new to us both? We can be adventurers together."

In response, he placed her hand over the lover's locket. His pulse thrummed beneath, strong and eager.

"My heart is yours. I love you, Angelica. I want to rub your hands when you're tired. I want to be your aural accompaniment for the rest of our lives. I want to read to you, kiss you, marry you—"

"*Yes.*" She wrapped her arms about his neck. "I love you, too. There's no one else I'd want to read me geology texts and odes to haggis. I cannot wait to explore the future at your side."

He swung her into a joyful circle and kissed her as though he'd never let her go.

EPILOGUE

June 1816
Spitalfields

"Mrs. Munroe will arrive at any moment," said Luther. "Where's her daughter's necklace?"

"Over here." Angelica slid the necklace into its case and handed it to her brother.

None of which interrupted Jonathan's flow as he read passages aloud from the latest Fit for a Duke catalogue in dramatic fashion.

"Double-breasted morning jacket!" He struck a flamboyant pose. "Seamless thigh padding!"

When they weren't tidying the shop, Esther and Florence pranced around their Uncle Jonathan, attempting to copy his absurd poses.

Angelica and Luther exchanged amused glances before returning their attention to their respective worktables.

Instead of purchasing her own window on

fashionable St. James, Angelica and Jonathan had decided instead to invest in expanding her brother's shop. Lending a hand whenever she was in town had become part of the pleasure.

The expanded shop was in constant motion. Fit for a Duke used Luther not only as a supplier, but also as a venue to display some of the most popular items in the catalogue. This increased the number of visitors to the shop, many of whom became jewelry clients as well.

When Angelica turned from the worktable, Jonathan was there at once to lift her hands in his and massage any tension away.

"You look beautiful," he murmured.

She gestured at her new pink frock. "You're just saying that because I'm wearing a prototype for the new Fit for a Duchess line."

"I would say it even if you weren't wearing anything." He gave her a wicked grin. "*Especially* then."

Her cheeks flushed hot. It was true. He showed her how beautiful she was every single day.

"Stop that," Luther called out without turning around from his workbench. "Don't you two have some random village you should be off visiting?"

"Not yet," Angelica replied happily. "You're saddled with us for six more days."

After which, they'd take the long way back to Cressmouth, recruiting new consignment partners in the Cotswolds or on the coast, and staying an extra week or two to enjoy the area.

She and Jonathan had found peace in a rhythm that worked for both of them. Most of their time was spent in Cressmouth, but their frequent visits to family or to Scotland always involved exploring new sights and shires along the way.

"Can I read from the catalogue now?" asked Esther.

"No!" Florence yanked it from her sister's hands. "It's my turn."

Jonathan pressed Angelica's palm to his lips, likely to hide his amusement. The girls were growing fast. Luther would have plenty of aural accompaniment, even after Angelica and Jonathan went away.

Angelica helped Jonathan make good use of his inheritance. They used half to create endowments for struggling businesses, so that others would not need to sign contracts like the one she'd had with Mr. Marlowe in order to have a future.

With the other half of the trust money, they made large donations to charities and abolitionist causes. They could not singlehandedly reinvent Britain, but they could make positive changes in a significant number of lives.

"Oh—and Mr. Rosenthal," said Luther. "Do you have the portrait for his locket?"

"I do." Jonathan kissed Angelica's cheek, then hurried to his work area, where he worked on

portrait commissions for eye miniatures whenever they were in London. His work had become
as popular as the lockets themselves. On the
counter was a register with a waiting list of satis-
fied customers, eager to add the crowning touch
to their purchase.

"Aunt?" came Florence's hesitant voice.

Angelica glanced down at her nieces, expecting to have to solve the argument of whose
turn it was to read aloud from the catalogue next.
One day, when they were a little older, they
would hand their brooms and rags to younger
cousins and learn to attend the shop's customers
instead.

She straightened one of the bows in her
niece's hair.

"I want to be a jeweler like you," said
Florence.

Esther turned to their father. "And I want to
be a jeweler like Papa."

"Will you teach us?" they asked at once.

Luther's flattered gaze met Angelica's over his
daughters' heads. They exchanged mischievous
grins.

He shook his head mournfully. "This is how it
starts."

But his eyes shone with pride.

"Of course you can be jewelers like us." Angelica exchanged a wink over her shoulder with
Jonathan, then turned to the girls. "Who wants to
go first?"

AUTHOR'S NOTE

*B*lack people have been living in England since the 1100s.

Numbers increased significantly from the 17th century onward, but the presence of Black people would not have been a surprising sight in Shakespeare's time, and certainly not unusual by the Regency era.

Jane Austen's unfinished manuscript *Sandition* features a sought-after mixed-race heroine. It is a truth universally acknowledged that an heiress from the West Indies in possession of a large fortune *must* be in want of a husband.

Long before slavery was abolished throughout the British Empire in 1833, free Black people lived a full range of lives, from paid servants to working class to fame and fortune. Musicians, sailors, preachers, businessmen, inventors, political activists. Black princes and dignitaries from African nations were celebrated in Polite Society.

There was still virulent racism, widespread disenfranchisement, and countless atrocities, despite one's status and supposed freedom. Even African princes could pay a white sea captain for transport to England only to find himself sold into slavery instead.

You may like to learn more about:

- Ignatius Sancho (composer, writer 1729-1780)
- Dido Elizabeth Belle (heiress 1761-1804)
- George Africanus (entrepreneur 1763-1834)
- Olaudah Equiano (writer & abolitionist 1745-1797)
- Bill Richmond (pugilist & pub owner 1763-1829)
- Joseph Emidy (musician & composer 1775-1835)
- George Bridgetower (virtuoso violinist 1778-1860)
- Cesar Picton (merchant & gentleman 1755-1836)
- Reasonable Blackman (silk merchant 1579-1592)
- Queen Charlotte (African-Portuguese ancestry 1744-1818)

For further reading, you may like *Black*

London by Gretchen Gerzina, which at the time of this writing can be downloaded for free from the Dartmouth College website.

Love talking books with fellow readers?

Join the ***Historical Romance Book Club*** for prizes, books, and live chats with your favorite romance authors:
   Facebook.com/groups/HistRomBookClub

And check out the official website for sneak peeks and more:
   www.EricaRidley.com/books

TEN DAYS WITH A DUKE

From a *New York Times* bestselling author: a second chances, enemies-while-lovers reunion romance where nothing is as it first appears, and everyone's motives are suspect...

Olive Harper's family has been feuding with the Westons for decades. The Westons' stud farm is the biggest, but the Harpers' is the most famous... and she's the sole heiress. Or *was*, until her father brokers a truce by offering the Weston heir the Harper farm. The only way to get it back is to marry the knave who kissed her and humiliated her, *twice*—or prove to her father that some rifts can never be healed.

Scholar and botanist Elijah Weston is dreadful at feuding. For one, he prefers horticulture to horses. For two, he's been desperately in love with his mortal enemy ever since he kissed her—and, yes, publicly destroyed her—all those years ago. When he's given ten days to win Olive's heart, he arrives with marriage license in hand. But where lies and double-crosses abound, how can lifelong rivals learn to trust their hearts?

A secret identities, forbidden love, opposites attract romance from a *New York Times* best-selling author: Why seduce a duke the normal way, when you can accidentally kidnap one in an elaborately planned heist?

Chloe Wynchester is completely forgettable -- a curse that gives her the ability to blend into any crowd. When the only father she's ever known makes a dying wish for his adopted family of orphans to recover a missing painting, she's the first one her siblings turn to for stealing it back. No one expects that in doing so, she'll also abduct a handsome duke.

Lawrence Gosling, the Duke of Faircliffe, is tortured by his father's mistakes. To repair his estate's ruined reputation, he must wed a highborn heiress. Yet when he finds himself in a carriage being driven hell-for-leather down the cobblestone streets of London by a beautiful woman who refuses to heed his commands, he fears his heart is hers. But how can he sacrifice his family's legacy to follow true love?

"Erica Ridley is a delight!"
    —Julia Quinn

"Irresistible romance and a family of delightful scoundrels... I want to be a Wynchester!"
    —Eloisa James

ACKNOWLEDGMENTS

As always, I could not have written this book without the invaluable support of my critique partner, beta readers, and editors. Huge thanks go out to Rose Lerner, Erica Monroe and Tessa Shapcott. You are the best!

Lastly, I want to thank the *12 Dukes of Christmas* facebook group, my *Historical Romance Book Club,* and my fabulous street team. Your enthusiasm makes the romance happen.

Thank you so much!

Erica Ridley is a *New York Times* and *USA Today* best-selling author of witty, feel-good historical romance novels, including the upcoming THE DUKE HEIST, featuring the Wild Wynchesters. Why seduce a duke the normal way, when you can accidentally kidnap one in an elaborately planned heist?

In the *12 Dukes of Christmas* series, enjoy witty, heartwarming Regency romps nestled in a picturesque snow-covered village. After all, nothing heats up a winter night quite like finding oneself in the arms of a duke!

Two popular series, the *Dukes of War* and *Rogues to Riches*, feature roguish peers and dashing war heroes who find love amongst the splendor and madness of Regency England.

When not reading or writing romances, Erica can be found riding camels in Africa, zip-lining through rainforests in Central America, or getting hopelessly lost in the middle of Budapest.

~

Let's be friends! Find Erica on:
www.EricaRidley.com